Jaeger

First published in Great Britain in 2024 by Black Shuck Books

All content © Simon Bestwick 2024

Cover design by WHITEspar
her in Cool it by WHITEspar
www.white-spar.co.uk

978-1-913038-80-9

First published in Great Britain in 2024 by Black Shuck Books

Cover design by WHITEspace
Set in Caslon by WHITEspace
www.white-space.uk

978-1-913038-80-9

Jaeger

by
Simon Bestwick

BLACK
SHUCK
BOOKS

Jaeger

by
Simon Bestwick

BLACK
SHUCK
BOOKS

For Anna Taborska

Drogi przyjacielu,
Utalentowany pisarz,
Delikatna dusza.

I'm good at leaving things behind. I have to be: I couldn't bear the weight of them otherwise.

I took so little when I left you behind, even less than I had brought with me. Money, papers and a gun was all I left with; that and the portrait of us both you bought me for our third anniversary. The two of us together, sealed in a pocket-sized oval frame of glass.

It's enough, anyway. I take you with me wherever I go. The memory of you. That first meeting in a crowded nurses' lounge; that last sight of you, stretched out on the living-room floor with a bullet in your head.

I meant to go somewhere new. When I walked out of the door, leaving your and Ulrich's bodies behind me, I was thinking of the countries I'd never set foot in. The continents, even: the Americas, Asia, Africa, Australasia... all the A's, basically. I had contact details for a pilot who'd fly me anywhere with no questions asked if I paid the right price. But despite my best intentions I found myself crossing the Channel by boat, then the continent by train. France, then Germany. And now I'm in Berlin.

The Grill Royal, to be precise, on the Friedrichstrasse, where I've just enjoyed a very nice meal in good company. She sits across the table from me, in a white sheath dress, wearing a necklace and gold earrings that subtly make you aware how much they cost without shoving it in your face, as only really tasteful jewellery can. Her name is Hanna, and her profile on the escort agency's website admitted to an age of twenty-nine. I think she's a little older, but it doesn't matter. She carries it well.

Most of all, she reminds me very much of you. It's an illusion, and it won't last: it isn't even fooling me now, but I hope it will later on, late into the night, when she and I are in bed together and I'm just on the edge of sleep. I hope it'll feel as though I'm with you again.

And I know that really isn't fair on Hanna, because she seems a genuinely nice woman. Good at her job, too, and no doubt with plenty to offer the man or woman of her choice whenever she's ready. Perhaps she already has someone, someone understanding about her profession: you and I were always strictly monogamous and I had no issue with that, but if I've learned anything in over a century of everlasting and near-invulnerable youth, it's the impermanence of physical things.

Although less tangible items such as commitment, in my experience, haven't always lasted either.

Hanna's talking. I shift my attention to her. It would be rude not to listen, especially not if I intend to sleep with her.

"I've got to admit," she's saying, in flawless German, "I was quite surprised when I saw you."

"Oh?" I say, and take a sip of coffee. I can guess what she's about to say.

"You didn't look as though you'd need, well—"

"To pay for it?" I ask.

She shrugs. "You could have your pick."

"Flattery will get you everywhere," I say.

"Now that, I'll drink to." She raises her coffee cup. I clink mine against hers and smile back at her. I like her, and not just because of her resemblance to you. She's intelligent, funny, charming... but then, you expect that from the better class of escort. All the same: she's a woman I could – no, I won't say come to love. I don't know when that will be possible for me again, if it ever will, not with you gone. She might be bones and dust before I feel capable of that again. And you're barely cold in the ground. But she's someone I'd want to spend time with, if I had the choice, and if I wasn't still trying to squirm out from under the weight of this grief.

I shouldn't be trying to rid myself of the pain. To think of it as something that could or should be shed so quickly insults your memory. In a way, the persistence of my grief is oddly comforting; I thought of ending my own life when you died, but couldn't, and wondered if immortality had robbed me – or was robbing me – of my ability to feel, which might be worse than death. But it seems not. Not yet, anyway.

All this has taken less than a second to think. It would be rude to drift away into reveries, and I badly want to sleep with Hanna. "I just wanted to keep things simple," I say. "Straightforward. I was in a relationship until recently. I'm not in a hurry to get back into one."

"There's such a thing as no strings attached."

"Often easier in theory than in practice." Should I tell her she reminds me of you? Best not. "I won't be in Berlin long. I just didn't want to spend the night alone."

"That's fair enough," she says. "So, what did you have in mind after this?"

"I have an apartment in Charlottenburg," I say. "We could go back there for a nightcap, if that's not a problem. Or if you'd rather, we can find a hotel." Going back to someone's home can be dangerous, after all; you never know what waits behind closed doors.

"Your apartment's fine," says Hanna. "I'm not worried about you." Is that meant as a compliment, or a veiled threat – that if I did turn out to have some malign agenda, she could deal with me? If she only knew. Nothing she's capable of doing would more than mildly inconvenience me if I meant her harm. Luckily for her, I don't.

She reaches out and covers my hand with hers. We exchanged a dry, formal kiss on each cheek at the beginning of the evening; this is our first real physical contact, and it sends a hot, electric thrill through me. That feeling of meeting someone new and knowing you'll soon be naked together; I haven't felt that in a long time. Then I remember that's because of all the happy years I spent with you, and the thrill is dampened.

"Valerie?" Hanna's frowning. "Are you okay?"

I nod. "Just an old memory."

"I'm sorry."

"It's not your fault."

"The ex?" she asks.

I nod.

"How long were you together?"

"Three years."

"Who broke up with who?"

"Neither," I say; I'm not going to lie about that part of it and cast either of us as the villain. "She died."

"Oh, shit. Valerie, I'm so sorry." Hanna puts a hand to her mouth.

"Don't worry about it. It's not something I advertise. I'm trying to move on."

"Some professional, right?" Hanna's embarrassed; she won't meet my eyes. "I promise you, I'm not normally so insensitive."

"You haven't been. So, would you like anything else?"

"I'm fine, thanks. Do you want to go back to yours? I mean, if you still want to—"

"I do." I cover her hand with mine. "Very much so."

There's a brief discussion of what is and isn't on the menu – the bedroom variety rather than the restaurant one – although I familiarised myself with that side of things earlier, and then I signal the waiter to bring the bill.

By the time the taxi drops us outside my apartment, we're giggling like schoolgirls. I've no idea why; I can't even remember what we were laughing at in the cab. It doesn't matter, anyway. It only matters that tonight, I'm not alone.

Arm in arm we cross the street. Streetlamps glow amid the rustling trees.

The air smells of blossom. It was winter when you died. I spent those months in the south of France, then made my way to Germany, and Berlin.

It's a beautiful city, under its well-concealed scars and the startling number of billboards advertising Dildo King. I was last here in 1945, playing cat and mouse with a Black Eagle called Czobor among the ruins. It was the year I finally tired of the ridiculous game and left Ulrich and the others behind. That was all I saw of the city in the Nazi era, thankfully; before that, I spent some months in it back in the Weimar days, exploring its decadent nightlife with Tibor.

Tibor. God, I miss him. Almost as much as I miss you.

I let myself into the apartment block and catch the elevator to the third floor. Hanna and I stand very close together, so close I can smell the rich coffee on her breath, so close we're almost touching, and yet we still don't kiss. I wait until the apartment door's closed behind us and the lights switched on low, and then I reach out for her, hesitantly. She takes charge from then on, pulling me close. The soft warmth of her body through the dress, so like and yet so unlike yours. Then her lips are on mine, her tongue in my mouth, and the next few minutes are a blur.

Then she breathes "I want you," and is leading me to the bed, and I go gladly, not even caring whether or not it's a lie. For the moment, at least, I'm happy to believe such falsehoods.

"I have to go," she says as she shakes me gently awake the next morning. Sunlight streams through the curtains; in trees outside, birds sing. "I promised I'd pick my little boy up."

I'd never have guessed she had children. But everyone has secrets, or at least aspects of their past not readily apparent to an observer. "Thank you for last night," I croak. My head aches and my tongue's thick. Too much wine.

"You're welcome." She kisses me lightly on the lips. "So, how long *will* you be in Berlin?"

"I haven't decided."

"Feel free to get in touch if you'd like to have dinner again." She smiles, brightly. "I had a lovely time. Oh, and there's a glass of water and some paracetamol next to the bed. *Tschüss, schätzchen.*"

She kisses a fingertip, touches it to my lips, and sashays to the door, handbag in one hand and shoes in the other. I sit up with a groan as the apartment door shuts behind her, then reach for the water and the pills.

Afterwards, I stumble to the bathroom because Nature calls, but before answering it I turn on the shower: the water can take a couple of minutes to heat up, and I want to step straight into it once I'm finished. It's perfect for reviving me after a heavy night, with powerful jets that pummel me awake and fill the bathroom with their roar.

That's why I don't hear the gunshots.

The first clue I have that anything's wrong comes as I'm sitting in the kitchen in a thick, comfortable towelling robe and sipping black coffee, when someone starts pounding on the apartment door.

Old instincts kick in. I'm probably worrying about nothing; Black Eagles and *Falkenjaeger* alike are relics of the past, like the Empire that spawned them. But nothing's ever quite forgotten; everything echoes, lingers, leaves its influence or taint. And despite the decades I spent trying to sever my connections with the person I was, all the old instincts were hiding away, waiting, for need and danger to reactivate them.

That's why the Roth-Steyr's hidden under the bed and loaded; all I need do is grab it as I pad through the apartment, pull back the bolt to chamber a round, and aim it towards the door. "Who's there?"

"*Polizei*," the answer comes.

I almost fire through the door, but I can always smell a cop, and that's what I smell now. Still: what do the police want with me? That's concerning in itself; my tracks ought to be well covered. I stow the Roth-Steyr under my robe and go to the door; if I can get out of whatever's next without being shot or marched away in handcuffs, I'll be all right.

There are two officers: a tall, gaunt black man and a small, birdlike woman. I relax at once: I was the only woman to be recruited by either side, and both the Black Eagles and the *Falkenjaeger* were thoroughly white. Austria-Hungary was ethnically diverse, but not to *that* extent.

"Yes?" I say.

"We're sorry to disturb you," says the man. "May we come in?"

"Of course." I've nothing to hide. Except that I do. But I have the Roth-Steyr, and even if they're armed they won't be able to harm me. Unless.

"Frau Steiner?" asks the woman.

"Yes." That's the name I rented this place under.

"I am Lieutenant Okelo," says the man. "This is Sergeant Trautmann. We need to ask you some questions."

"Of course. About what?"

"I'm afraid there was an incident outside this building earlier," says Trautmann. They take turns speaking, like a double act.

"What sort of incident?"

"You didn't hear?" Okelo asks.

"I was out last night with a friend." It seems the easiest way to describe Hanna for now. "I had... a little too much to drink. I've been feeling a bit delicate this morning."

"There was a shooting," says Trautmann.

My first reaction is surprise: that doesn't happen, not in leafy Charlottenburg. Kreuzberg, maybe, with its mix of hipsters and even less savoury characters. There's a cold twitching in my stomach. Another kind of unease. Outside this building: outside the place I happen to be. "A shooting?"

Okelo takes something from his pocket. "Do you know this woman?" An identity card of some kind, with blood on it; blood, and a photo of Hanna.

I tell the truth; we had dinner together yesterday evening, and she spent the night here. Yes, I knew she was an escort. I've broken no laws.

I'm questioned about my background, and my presence in Berlin. I tell them I've lived in France for several years; now I've come back to Germany, perhaps to visit, perhaps to settle. Half-truths and lies, but the records and documents I'm using should stand up to cursory inspection. A deeper look, and cracks might start to show, but the important thing's to remain at liberty for now.

And to determine what happened to Hanna. Or more specifically, whether it has anything to do with me.

She's still alive, thank whatever gods exist. (I may have glimpsed a god once, over a century ago, but

I doubt the one I saw would ever intercede on our behalf – at least, not in any way we'd want.) A man fired a machine-pistol at her from a car parked across the street; she was hit twice in the chest and again in the head. The headshot went astray, only grazing her skull. The chest wounds sent her to the Franziskus-Krankenhaus – the nearest A&E – in a critical condition. No visitors allowed.

Nothing in Hanna's past suggests, so far, why anyone would want her dead. If it did it would be a relief, but I know it won't.

When the police have gone – having told me not to leave Berlin without authorisation – I sit on the bed, the Roth-Steyr on my lap, tracing the pistol's lines with my fingertips.

A machine-pistol, Okelo said. Trautmann frowned when he did, as if he'd given too much away. Some sleek, compact weapon easily hidden under a jacket, beside which my Roth-Steyr seems crude and unsophisticated. Nonetheless, the same function is served.

At least Hanna's still alive. A sloppy job; they had the front of the building staked out and were waiting in the car, but they fired fast, panicked and fled. They didn't even confirm the kill. Tibor and I once carried out a similar mission, armed only with our pistols, but we brought our quarry down and Tibor covered me when I went in to make sure of the job with two rounds to the head. If you're going to kill somebody, do it right.

The police will be running their forensic tests now, like Mr Veale back in Manchester would. I wonder how Mr Veale is, how he received the news of your death and my vanishing. And my old boss,

Dr Sharma, too. I've purposely avoided looking at any of the news coverage of your death. I will have come under suspicion: of course I will, having disappeared like that. I hope neither Mr Veale nor Dr Sharma believe I could have hurt you. But no one can really know anybody, can they? You thought you knew me. What secrets might you have disclosed to me in time that I'll never hear now, or taken to your grave even if we'd spent a century together?

If I could lay hands on the bullets that hit Hanna, I could answer the most important question of all. Nothing in their laboratories could tell them. But I could, and instantly.

I could tell them who the bullets were really meant for.

But I think I already know.

And that's the sloppiest part of all.

I take a deep breath and let it out. Is this connected to Ulrich and the rest? It doesn't seem likely; all the time I laid low in France, there was never a hint of danger. Although it's always possible. While I and others gave up the causes we were supposed to fight for throughout eternity – in a matter of decades, in my case – others clung steelily to it. Like Ulrich, although it drove him mad. And Tibor and Erick followed him. Tibor I understand least of all; even when I last saw him, the madness of it had never eaten into his soul as it had Ulrich's. He remained his old irreverent self, laughing it at all. Perhaps that was why: it was all a joke, all absurd, so why not carry on?

Some might not know – or believe – I've renounced the fight. Or care. Others still might regard me as a traitor, as Ulrich did. It's entirely possible that ever since Manchester I've been hunted. But it's just as likely I've unwittingly strayed into some other immortal's stamping-ground: another survivor of the Sindelar Gate who's made Berlin his home, and, territorial as a dog, readied his fangs in response to my intrusion.

Perhaps. Perhaps. There's no certainty to it.

What I *am* certain of is that something new's happened here. That puts me on unfamiliar, treacherous ground, and I don't intend to stay on it any longer than I must.

Okelo told me not to leave Berlin without permission. Sadly, I must disobey him. Not that I need his understanding, but you'd hope in Germany, more than any other European nation, they'd know the importance of disobedience now and then, and how lethal unquestioning obedience can be.

If I stay, the authorities may detain me; they might also begin to chisel away at my assumed identity, and that would never do. But far more to the point, whoever tried to kill me this morning will almost certainly try again. And the next time they won't confuse me with the girl who shared my bed.

I get up, throw off the towelling robe, and dress. Plain clothes, the kind that shouldn't draw attention, including a light sweater bulky enough to hide the two money-belts. I converted a substantial chunk of assets into ready cash in the form of euros. Just in case. Far less traceable than credit cards.

Other than that? Passports, ID cards. Those in the name of Valerie Steiner are just one of three sets I carry with me; if necessary, that identity can vanish within five minutes of my leaving here. A few small bottles of hair dye. And the gun, of course. The gun and the bullets.

That's all I need. I left our home in Manchester with less.

I let myself out of the apartment, head downstairs and step outside into the sunshine. Fresh spring air, full of promise and brightness. On the pavement, the red stain where Hanna nearly died, markings to show where bullet cases fell. My breath catches. She's an innocent, after all. But they're always the ones who suffer.

I start walking, keeping my pace slow and unhurried, and wait to see who follows.

I catch a bus to the Tiergarten, potter around for an hour or two, then go for lunch. The Café Einstein, on Kurfürstenstrasse, is a fine old place in the Viennese style; the influence shows in the cuisine and – better still – the coffee. I order Wiener schnitzel with potatoes, suspecting I'll need the energy. I also order an *Einspänner* – coffee topped with whipped cream, an old favourite of mine from the Vienna days – and iced water to drink with the meal. No booze; it takes a lot to get me drunk, but I want a clear head.

By then I've established a cop's tailing me, which is no surprise. Okelo and Trautmann aren't stupid; their very first assumption would be I'm involved. They're the least of my worries, but distractions can be fatal. Fortunately I learned how to shake a tail years ago, and I'm both relieved and depressed – as always when I call on these old skills – to lose this one within fifteen minutes of leaving the Einstein. Surveillance technology's come a long way, though, so I'd best not be overconfident.

I wander from shop to shop, buying a new jacket and surreptitiously ditching the old one. Then a hat. A pair of glasses. Small things, altering my appearance just a little each time. A backpack, too, to hold a few other purchases.

Having done what I need to, I ramble about the city; losing myself briefly in the crowds of tourists at the Brandenburger Tor, I walk past the fragment of the Wall left standing, down Zimmerstrasse, and across Friedrichstrasse where Checkpoint Charlie once stood.

It's the first time I've ever gone near the Wall's remains. I missed that whole era. I remember the Communist revolutions that rocked Europe at the end of the Great War. Back then I was too much a prisoner of my upbringing, too grief-stricken at my brothers' deaths, to have any sympathy with the Reds or Anarchists. I needed something familiar to cling to. Even my rebellion was an act of reaction: becoming an agent for the *Evidenzbüro*, demanding to walk the Sindelar Gate with my brother. If I'd known then what I know now—

What would I have done? I ask myself, wandering south over Prinzenstrasse. Joined the Reds? Part of me would like to think so – see through all that old order's rottenness and falsity, tear it down to build a better, more just world. But then, that's hardly what happened, as this old wound's remains testify. Could things ever have gone differently? New worlds are always born in blood. But that hope, that ideal, soured and turned to bitter greyness, purged of all humanity even as it killed, grinding away the souls of those inside it and leaving only scars behind, like this broken wall.

Thankfully, not a world I knew. By the time of the Cold War, my part in the *Geheimkrieg* – the 'secret war' – was over, and I was trying to redeem my past with whatever healing or kindness I was capable of. I finished with the war here in Berlin, or the pulverised ruin of it that remained in 1945. But that wasn't my Berlin, either; my Berlin was another city entirely.

I leave the Wall behind. Before I leave Berlin, I want to revisit a place that holds happier memories. I catch a bus to Schöneberg.

I never saw Berlin before the Great War. That posturing idiot of a Kaiser, the strutting soldiers, and my grandfather's tales of the Six Weeks' War between the Empire and Prussia and our crushing defeat at the Battle of Sadowa (he was, in retrospect, a very sore loser,) put me off. But after the Great War, it was a different world…

Berlin! Berlin in 1925 – the Jazz Age, the chaotic, stormy heyday of the Weimar Republic, that fragile, tottering democracy like a woman balancing on a fence, hungry wolves snapping on each side – Fascist and Communist, Black and Red, Nazi and KPD. In retrospect it could never have lasted, but while it did, freedoms denied for decades, if not centuries, were granted – or licenced, at least. A licentious city, in the best sense of the term.

We were on the trail of a group of Black Eagles; Ulrich and the others divided into pairs to search the country methodically, state by state, while Tibor and I 'held the fort' in the capital. When they came back a few weeks later, the floor of the apartment we'd rented was strewn with empty champagne bottles and cigarette butts and I was in bed with three lusty and inventive German girls, while Tibor was in his with two strapping lads – one, he later claimed, from the Nazi SA and the other from the Communist RFB.

Ulrich was furious, but how could we have resisted such temptation? By then, we'd spent five years wading through chaos and destruction in search of our enemies: Berlin offered the pair of us opportunities we weren't about to deny. Ulrich was too much the warrior-ascetic to give way to his fleshly appetites – it might have done him good if he had – although I expect the others indulged themselves on their travels. I hope so, anyway: two of us were dead within two years – shot in the back by a Black Eagle called Janáček, who slipped away like a ghost.

(His ex-comrade Varga told me Janáček lived another seventy years, then went and blew his brains out in 1997: the year of Hale-Bopp and Heaven's Gate, the Rwandan Genocide and Princess Di, New Labour, Cool Britannia, the first *Harry Potter* book. A world away from where we'd started. Maybe that was why.)

Yes, Berlin in '25 was a hell of place to be queer in, one way or the other, and we gorged ourselves as at a feast. Vienna before the War had had its moments, if you knew where to go, but compared to Berlin it was like the difference between *Einspänner* and *Linzer torte* in Griensteidl's coffee house and… well… a three-course meal at the Grill Royal.

I remember my thrilled astonishment when I first read magazines like *Frauenliebe* and *Die Freundin*: magazines about women who loved – who *fucked* – women, *by* women who fucked women, *for* women who fucked women. And then we discovered the clubs; dozens of clubs for men like Tibor, women like me.

Tibor sometimes frequented the bigger, fancier transvestite clubs like the Eldorado, which drew huge gay crowds along with artists, authors and celebrities, but more often liked to trawl smaller, more 'lower-class' establishments like Noster's Cottage, a homely little pub near Hallesches Tor where handsome boys with unbuttoned shirts and rolled-up sleeves waited patiently to be picked up.

The best-known lesbian club back then was the Chez Ma Belle Soeur on Charlottenburg's Marburger Strasse, but that wasn't my scene. Greek-style frescos and low-lit booths for couples, soft music setting the mood for romance: I didn't want that. I still sort-of believed in my mission in those days; enough to have a sense of duty. No time for love or commitment: I had seven years' worth of bottled-up lust in need of an outlet. Luckily the Berlin scene offered as much variety for women as it did for men, and I soon found ones where you could met a girl – or girls, if you were greedy, like me – who just wanted a good time. Who wanted, for one night, not to feel like a freak, to know there were others like them, and find joy in what they were...

Schöneberg: the heart of gay Berlin, then and now. I wander along Motzstrasse to the corner where the Eldorado stood. It's a restaurant now. I stand outside for a moment, but don't go in, remembering Tibor and I staggering out of there the night before Ulrich and the others came back, Tibor with his boys hanging on one arm, me with my three girls on mine and each of us with our free arm wrapped around the other.

And all of us with our heads thrown back, singing *The Lavender Song*:

"*Ours is a world of romance and delights,*
While theirs is nothing but banality,
Our greatest treasures are these lavender nights,
Where we're only who we want to be…"[1]

My eyes sting. Memory's cruel sometimes. I move on; best not to draw attention.

I loved the Eldorado. It welcomed gay women too, so I'd often go with Tibor – him in rouge and lipstick, me in top hat, tux and waistcoat, a cigarette hanging from my lips. We rarely went to our respective beds alone, and rarely with the same partner or partners. When we weren't in bed with our latest lovers, or recovering the morning after, I can't remember what we talked about, only that I laughed so much, so hard I thought I'd die for lack of breath. And that I felt I'd glimpsed the kind of life I wanted, although the sexual gymnastics I indulged in then feel too much like hard work now. Perhaps I've grown staid. But then, with you, I never felt I needed anything else. I think – before I met you – it was the happiest time of my life. I didn't want love then. Not then. But later it was a different story, just like it is now.

One fantasy I entertained throughout our life together was that I'd somehow find Tibor again, so you could meet him. The two people I loved most:

---

[1] A rather free, but quite lovely, translation one of the drag queens at the Eldorado gave an Englishwoman I met, one night at about four in the morning. We were very drunk, but it was a wonderful evening, not least because the Englishwoman and I ended up in bed. But that's another story. V von B-V.

my dearest friend and my soulmate. (They laugh at the idea of soulmates now, yet you and I seemed so perfect together. But how true could that have been, when I'd never told you who I really was, never did till it was too late and I was breathing the words in your dead ear? Even the idea of souls is passé now. Still, I've seen the pendulum swing before, ideas and discoveries going in and out of fashion. Even if what I saw when I walked the Sindelar Gate was hard to reconcile with the Church's teachings; even if, assuming I had a soul to begin with, I've no idea if I still do.)

But you'd have loved Tibor, and he'd have loved you. Or perhaps that's just wishful thinking; he stayed with Ulrich nearly eighty years after all, fighting the secret war. Even for an immortal, time wreaks changes crueller than we'd ever suspect when young.

God, I miss you both. I don't think I'll ever stop.

If someone wants me dead, maybe I should oblige them. It would be an end to that pain, at least. (Or not, depending on what's waiting on the other side of death.) A bleak thought, and one I need to guard against. If I'm to die, it'll be when and where I choose. The Roth-Steyr can do that for me whenever I like. But *I'll* decide, not them.

From Schöneberg I make my way to Kreuzberg. I must have walked for miles by now, but my feet barely ache at all: I feel energised, more alive than in months. I also realise I've acquired another tail, or more precisely three, as I make my way under the bright-painted tower blocks along the graffitied concrete channel of Kotbusser Tor. I'm in a seedier part of the city now, with more opportunities for the assassin.

Because *these* men aren't police. Under his bulky jacket, one carries a machine-pistol; another has an automatic in his waistband: nickel-plated, a poseur's gun. Besides, as I said, I can smell cops, however well-disguised. Back in the '80s, one joined a left-wing group I was with in Britain: he said and did all the right things, but I suspected him from the start, even without proof. I warned a friend of mine about him when he began charming her, but she wouldn't believe me; we fell out, in fact. They got together – had a child – and, years later, it came out he'd been one of the undercover detectives the Met planted in 'subversive' groups, lying their way into beds and hearts, building relationships on crueller, more cynical lies than any I ever told you. Those were bad enough, but at least I loved – love – you. Men like that are rapists by stealth, nothing more.

Yes, I can smell cops, and these are… something different. But who? What? They're neither *Falkenjaeger*, nor Black Eagles. We only knew the codenames of the other *Falkenjaeger* units, communicating with them by dead-drop, but we knew the personnel and I memorised the face of every fellow immortal, friend or foe, before we set out on the Black Eagles' trail. And these are amateurs, compared to those I've dealt with. Although I suppose their skills could have rusted with disuse. I've always worried mine did. Certainly Varga got the drop on me easily enough back in Manchester; would have killed me had the war not been over for him too. But the next immortal I faced was Ulrich. He had the drop on me as well. And I shot him in the throat, then put a pillow over his face and blew his brains out. What did I feel? I still don't know. I shut it away in a steel box then and there, the better to grieve for you. And then I ran, and haven't stopped.

Even if there were three immortals I didn't know by sight, would they risk themselves like this? Perhaps. Three to one might seem good odds, after all. And they have a machine-pistol and a modern automatic, plus who knows what else, against one antique cavalry pistol.

It all depends, in this case, on the ammunition. If these are just ordinary men, with ordinary bullets, none of their firepower will help them. But why would ordinary men with ordinary bullets want me dead?

Questions without answers for now: I need, in the words of Conan Doyle's detective, more data.

I keep walking, turning down this street and along that, but speed up. The big danger is they'll try to box me in. One gets behind me, one ahead; the other keeps to the side. Spread out enough that I might get one of them, maybe two, but not the third. Not in time.

I weave at random, trying to remember my way around the city from past visits, tourist guides and Google Maps. Luckily my bump of direction isn't bad. Another skill drummed into me at Aehrenbach by that ruthlessly efficient old tyrant Sándor Horváth, trainer of officer-cadets and *Falkenjaeger*, dog-murderer and all-round bastard: how to read a map and apply the knowledge to the terrain at ground level. So I'm soon weaving a suitably crooked path across Berlin.

It's quickly clear these are ordinary mortal men; sustaining the pace is too big a challenge for them. I glimpse red faces, and hear – in the quieter moments, over the growl of traffic and the muttering of passers-by – the sound of huffing, wheezing breaths. I glimpse Machine-Pistol reach under his jacket, only for Nickel-Plating to catch his arm and mutter in his ear.

But mortal or not, the ammunition is what counts tonight. I need to finish this, but it has to be on my terms, not theirs. So I pretend to panic and bolt across the road down a side-street, towards an abandoned building. From behind I hear their startled, breathless cries and the clatter of their footsteps as they give chase.

I run past the building's barred main door, down an alley at the side; wrap my coat around my arm, break a window, crawl through.

The room's dark. I can't see what state it's in, but that doesn't matter. I crouch by the window, moving just to the side, and draw the Roth-Steyr.

Nickel-Plating is first, the torch clipped beneath his gun's barrel sweeping back and forth across a stripped office space – over a desk and rusty filing-cabinet – to the open door at the far end. Checking out the whole room, all except that little patch of shadow immediately below him, because of course I must be running, trying to hide myself in the building's depths.

He jumps through, landing inches away. Surely he feels my presence, so close to him? But apparently not – off he goes, sprinting across the room. Another man lands in front of me: younger, lean and athletic, clutching a silenced target pistol. And finally, heaving himself up into the window-frame, a squat, heavy man, wheezing for breath. When I look up, I see the machine-pistol hanging on a sling inside his jacket, a thick red face above it. And then he looks down.

He sees me, but too late: I ram the Roth-Steyr into his groin and fire. He drops like a weighted sack: doesn't even scream.

As Silencer turns, I shoot him in the temple. This second shot, unmuffled, rings loud in the narrow space. Nickel-Plating's gun comes up; I take aim and shout

"Drop—" but he's already fired. The bullet whips past my ear, punching into the wall. Dust and splinters; reflexively, I fire twice. Nickel-Plating hits the wall behind him; falls to his knees, then onto his side.

Fuck.

I scrabble in the dirt for my bullet-casings, listening out for footsteps. I have to move quickly, stopping only to confirm Machine-Pistol's as dead as the others.

I should be glad and nothing more – three-to-one odds and I'm still here – but I wanted information, not notches on my gun, and I know no more now than previously.

Then something occurs to me. I take Silencer's pistol and shove it in my other coat pocket, climb back out of the window and run to the far end of the alley into an adjoining street. And then I'm on the move again.

At least I put my gloves on, I tell myself as I nurse a cup of black coffee in shaking fingers at a table outside a little café. No fingerprints. But *Christ*, if I was seen…

Breathe in. Breathe out. Having calmed myself, I slip Silencer's gun from my coat pocket and study it under the table. A .22 target pistol, but it isn't the gun I'm interested in. I pull back the bolt, ejecting the chambered round, and palm the bullet. And even before I pocket the gun again, I have an answer.

———

When I first saw the circle, I despaired; even after all my training, I thought there was no way I'd ever memorise so intricate a design. Especially not when the slightest deviation or error could be catastrophic.

"Don't worry," said Siczynski. "It's really not so difficult."

I tried not to look too doubtful. We all did: Ulrich and I; Erick and Tibor; Stefan, Albin and Mathias. Seven who'd walked the Sindelar Gate and lived.

Siczynski was the polar opposite of Horváth. Slow, patient and kind – you'd never have thought there was a war on, let alone that the Empire was disintegrating around us – soft-spoken and shy, with gold-rimmed glasses he had to keep pushing up the bridge of his beaky nose. Only in his mid-twenties, he was already going bald, his remaining hair touched with grey. A family trait, or maybe he'd just had a bad war.

An armourer by trade, he knew guns and ammunition, albeit with a fine distaste for what they actually did. He didn't belong in the Army: he'd have been happier as a watchmaker – or a toymaker, better still. I could easily see that. A builder of ingenious clockwork toys.

To Siczynski, guns and bullets were simply matters of physics and engineering. That was how he dealt with it: how he avoided having to contemplate what they were actually for, what happened when the equations and formulae were translated into action, what the correct functioning of the gears, bolts and springs, the strikers, extractors and magazines, would result in when aimed at a human target. What *was* a man like him doing in the Army? He could have done so much else, so much better. It must have been a sense of duty: after the Empire broke up, he became a Polish citizen and joined *their* Army. Spent his whole life in the military, for all that he despised it, till he was rounded up by the Nazis, gassed and burned to ash. Just another life, used up and thrown away by a cause that didn't deserve it…

A blessed relief after Horváth, as I said. But Horváth's tactics wouldn't have worked with what Siczynski was teaching us anyway. Everything had to be laid out very precisely – in exactly the right order and aligned to the correct point of the compass; some sigils drawn from left to right, others from right to left. Even after the Sindelar Gate, it seemed impossibly complex.

"Don't worry, Countess," he said. He always addressed us by our titles, with none of Horváth's mockery, however often Tibor and I asked him to use our first names. "It's no different from a pistol: just so many interlocking parts. Bewildering at first, but once you're familiar with it…" He clicked his fingers. "Bagatelle."

I've never got *that* blasé about it, since in over a century I've used the ritual he taught us no more than three times. But I learned what I needed to: how to break the complex ceremony down into a sequence of simpler, easily-memorised tasks, and the mnemonics that enabled us to remember the correct sequences.

All of which helped me to focus, to concentrate: the most important part of any magical ritual. Focusing the will in order to amplify it, or to invoke some higher (or lower) entity's aid. I'm not sure *what* Siczynski's ritual invoked, whether the knowledge of how to kill those who'd walked the Sindelar Gate came from the same source as the Gate itself or somewhere else entirely. Tibor – ever curious and irreverent and always up for any prospect of sexual shenanigans (a lovely word, that, one I never learned until I came to live in Britain but which seems almost tailor-made for Tibor Thököly) found ample opportunity for the latter in the antics of so many 'magickal' practitioners

– like that hideous fraud Crowley – and threw himself into them with gay (pun most definitely intended; this is Tibor I'm talking about, after all) abandon in the name of 'research,' to better arm us against the enemy. But though he sucked and fucked till he was sore and walking bandy-legged, he never found any symbols, words or rites remotely resembling those Siczynski taught us. So we never knew whether we were summoning up devils, calling down angels, or slipping some other, nameless entity in through a sideways door. Didn't matter which: Emperor Karl had secured a Papal Dispensation for those who'd walked the Gate on his behalf, indemnifying us against suicide – our only way of leaving this world if the Black Eagles didn't kill us – or the use of whatever rites we found it necessary to deploy.

Having built your circle and 'prepared the way,' (a good hour's work in itself,) you placed a single bullet in the circle's centre and prayed (or more accurately incanted) over it for an hour, after which you could begin again with another round. You can see why I only went through the ritual three times. Whenever I did, the rest of the group stood guard, ensuring no one took advantage of my preoccupation to attack me. I could sleep for two hours at a time before resuming the incantations; any longer and the circle's power faded, and I'd have to begin all over again. Jesus wept. And quite possibly His Mother and a host of saints, too.

But only this way, bullet by bullet, could a *Falkenjaeger* replenish her stores of ammunition, so I always strove to do so with as many the bullets as I could, to postpone the need to do so again as long as possible. Another reason both we and the Black

Eagles used our old service guns, however archaic they became with the passing years: we'd often carry a second, more up-to-date pistol, loaded with ordinary ammunition for ordinary enemies, so as not to waste bullets like this on a mere mortal.

Two pistols: different makes, models and calibres, and usually different sizes too, so you wouldn't use the wrong weapon in a pinch. I favoured a little .25 Ortgies automatic back in the old days. Smaller than the Roth-Steyr and easily hidden, despite its tiny calibre it was a fine, accurate pistol and I was a good enough shot to make it count when I had to use it.

There was another test, though, although there wasn't always time to do it if you were in a rush, and it was useless if you wore gloves. Press a correctly-prepared bullet against the skin of one who'd walked the Gate, and they'd feel a slight but very distinctive burning sensation – and, in darkness, the bullet, where it pressed against the skin, gave off a faint blue glow.

Which the bullet from Silencer's target pistol is doing now, when I open my hand under the table. But I'd already felt it burning against my palm when I caught it in my fist.

So, that question's answered: Silencer was loaded for bear, or rather *Falkenjaeger*. I'd be surprised if I got a different result from the bullets in Machine-Pistol's or Nickel-Plating's guns.

Whether *they* knew there was anything special about their ammunition I've no way of knowing: interrogating the dead sadly isn't among my skills. God knows I've spoken to you countless times since leaving Manchester, but I've never heard a whisper in reply.

I pocket the bullet and order another coffee, along with a pastry. I haven't heard any sirens, so – thank God – it looks as though the gunshots didn't bring anybody running. But how long before Lieutenant Okelo and Sergeant Trautmann come looking for me again? I kept my gloves on, but I might have been seen. Or what if I've left some trace of DNA somewhere? Or –

Besides, the machine-pistol's almost certainly the one that cut Hanna down outside my flat. So I've exacted some measure of justice on her behalf, but if any witnesses or CCTV cameras glimpsed me in the vicinity, Okelo and Trautmann would be fools not to make the connection.

That said, the police are the least of my worries in Berlin. A good thing, then, that I left the flat prepared.

I drop the target pistol, silencer and bullet down a sewer grating, then take a bus to Neukölln and book into a suitably sleazy hotel. It's the kind of place where you pay by the hour, which is exactly what I need.

In the room, I empty my rucksack out onto the bed and quickly undress, stuffing the discarded clothing into the sack to get rid of later. I gather the items from the rucksack: Doc Marten boots, ripped jeans, a t-shirt with the name of a rock band on it, a spike-studded leather jacket. A slightly cliché image, but that's all to the good.

I break out one of the bottles of hair dye, apply it and pace the room in my underwear, waiting for it to dry. Sometimes I wish I still smoked. Or at least had a bottle of brandy to hand. But, as before, that wouldn't be wise. I'm not clear of danger yet, won't be until I'm out of Berlin and perhaps not even then. So I stop pacing and rock back and forth on the bed, facing the door, my hand on the Roth-Steyr, before remembering the window behind me and turning to face that instead, convinced they'll come at me that way.

But no one does. Even so, it's an effort to get myself back into the bathroom to finish the job. My back will be turned and the noise could cover the sound of an approaching killer...

I shake my head, stand up and go into the bathroom with the pistol and one more item from my earlier shopping spree: a pair of battery-powered hair clippers. My hair's now a glorious shade of neon pink, something I haven't tried before and would love to admire in all its splendour at length, but that'll have to wait: I shave off everything, except for a narrow strip extending from my hairline to the nape of my neck.

That done, I can't hold back the paranoia any longer and grab the Roth-Steyr before doing a sweep of the room. Can't see anything. Can't hear anything. Still safe. Maybe.

I'm tired, my back and neck are itchy with bits of freshly-cut hair, and my feet have now decided to start throbbing. I'd love a shower, but daren't risk it. I towel myself instead to get rid of the stray hairs, sweep up and bag the debris: they'll probably find the odd pink-coloured hair on the floor to check for DNA, but there's no sense making it easy for them.

I dress; finally, I apply my make-up. Kohl eyeliner and black lipstick; vivid green and purple eyeshadow. When I look in the mirror, a leathered-up punkette with a day-glo Mohican glares back. I look younger: a rebellious teenager instead of a woman in her late twenties. All to the good. The less I resemble the woman they're looking for, the better.

The rucksack looks far more at home on this new me. The leather jacket, a size too large, hangs down below my hips, hiding the Roth-Steyr in the back of my waistband.

I slip out of the room and go downstairs. In the lobby, the desk clerk has her nose in the latest issue of *Bild* and doesn't even see me slip out into the night crowds, weaving through the late-night drunks to the Hauptbahnhof. I get into a fast walking rhythm and the pain in my feet fades to a distant ache.

At the station, I check the train times: there's a EuroCity leaving for Prague in the next quarter-hour. Perfect. I buy a ticket, board the train and find a table with a window seat: might as well enjoy the view in full. It's been a long time since I travelled by rail in Europe. I look out over the neat, clean platform. The carriages are spacious, with legroom you could only dream of on a train in Britain, but I still find myself missing the comparative scruffiness of the British railways, because my memories of them are all tied up with you. Everything comes back to you. Always does.

The train groans into life; I breathe out and close my eyes as the EuroCity gathers speed.

I didn't start running without a destination in mind. There's a place I've wanted to see again for a long time, assuming it still exists. And there's no time like the present.

For me, in fact, there may be no time *other* than the present, depending on who wants me dead. With luck, it was just a Black Eagle, still looking over his shoulder a century later, and not one of my former comrades...

In any case, while I can, I'm going home.

———

Later, when the train pulls out of Dresden, rolling on into the night, I slip away to the bathroom for another change of appearance.

Off goes the make-up. The jacket and t-shirt vanish into the rucksack, but I keep the boots and jeans, putting on a linen shirt and leather waistcoat – more souvenirs from my last Berlin shopping spree – and a pair of round-framed spectacles with thick fake lenses. The clippers pare away the last of my hair – farewell, Mohican, we barely knew thee – and I wrap a silk scarf around my newly-bald head.

A touch of make-up, to get the weary, haggard look I want – although it doesn't take that much effort as I'm fighting the urge to sleep with all I have. When I look in the mirror after rinsing away the cut hair, the teen punkette is now a drawn and pallid cancer patient, looking far closer to forty than the twenty-nine years I'd lived when I walked the Sindelar Gate. I select a suitable fake ID and leave the bathroom, finding a new seat in the next carriage.

Hopefully that'll throw Okelo and Trautmann off the scent, for a little while at least. I settle back in my seat, and despite my resolve I close my eyes for a moment, then wake up as the train's arriving in Prague.

———

Despite the combined efforts of the Third Reich and the USSR, I can still recognise much of the Prague I knew before the Habsburgs fell, and she remains one of Europe's most beautiful cities. At last, I relax. I've either thrown my pursuers off the scent, or they've no interest in following me beyond their territory. I can plan my next move at leisure; it's a big world, and I've plenty of time...

Although I miss the urgency of having something to keep ahead of. Funny, but not wholly surprising. Adrenaline plays its part; besides, you value most what you're likeliest to lose. In all the lives I've had, I was happiest when I could live as an ordinary human soul, with the same limits as the rest. But it could never last; I always had to move on. And once again, assuming souls exist, I don't even know if I still have one.

Being here reminds me of how I ached to go to Vienna – home, after all those years of wandering – with you. Assuming you were still with me, of course, because by then I'd have told you all my secrets. Prague would have been a pleasant stop along the way, and in Vinohrady there's a vibrant gay scene: I book into the La Fenice hotel there, and sip coffee on the balcony, imagining us walking through the streets arm in arm. Something else Ulrich robbed me of; the thought sends the knowledge of your death shearing through me afresh, and in that moment I could happily kill my brother a second time. And a third, a fourth, a fifth. I don't know how many times would finally be enough, or if there'd ever be a limit to them.

I have a few quiet drinks in Vinohrady – nightclubs no longer being my thing – relaxing in the Q-Café, the Bourgeois Pig and the Saints Bar. I'm flattered to get a few come-hither looks, but go back to my hotel alone. Thinking of coming here with you only reminds me that now I never can, and much as I might wish for some companionship I don't want another Hanna on my conscience. Which reminds me...

I buy a cheap laptop and try to check up on her; as far as I can tell, nothing's changed and Hanna remains in critical condition at the Franziskus-Krankenhaus. I log out feeling a cruel stab of guilt and the strangest urge to pray for her safety, something I thought I'd long left behind. (Existence or non-existence aside, there's also the question of whether God would listen to anything I had to say.)

At least my would-be killers, having realised their mistake, have left her alone. No point silencing someone with nothing to say, or threatening someone who means nothing to me. After all, she shouldn't; she was – is – an escort and it was a one-night stand. A *Falkenjaeger* would be ruthless; a *Falkenjaeger* wouldn't care. If they had a gun to Hanna's head, a *Falkenjaeger* wouldn't even look away when they pulled the trigger.

But I haven't been a *Falkenjaeger* in almost eighty years. If they did threaten her to draw me out into the open, I honestly can't be sure what I'd do; nor do I want to consider it. Her resemblance to you only complicates things; I might act differently if the similarity I picked her for wasn't there. Or not. I don't want another innocent life on my conscience. It's annoying, sometimes, to have one.

I dismiss such thoughts, along with any others relating to Hanna, as best I can. That's done now. Berlin is over; I got away, and wasn't followed. It's time to carry on.

I spend a few more days in Prague, sightseeing like any old tourist – Prague Castle, the Old Town Square and the mediaeval Astronomical Clock's hourly animated display. But the Old Town's winding streets are packed with tourists, rowdy with the noise of the shops and the fast-food places that fill the air with the smell of kebabs and *trdelnik*; the Charles Bridge, with its statues of Catholic saints, is almost impossible to walk through. On Karlova Street there are shops selling babushka dolls and Red Army hats.

I need something else, I realise. Peace, perhaps. Quiet. Perhaps that's why I get the urge to visit a church, even though I don't believe. Although raised a Catholic, it's the Orthodox Cathedral of Saints Cyril and Methodius I'm drawn to, catching the tram to Jiraskovo Namesti and walking the rest of the way.

At first it seems like a poor choice for anyone in search of quiet: on the busy four-lane outside the Cathedral, cars roar back and forth and the air's thick with exhaust fumes, but when I slip in through the main doors, a kind of stillness enfolds me nonetheless.

This is where the Czech Resistance fighters who assassinated Reinhard Heydrich made their last stand. Seven of them held the church for four hours, finally killing themselves to avoid capture and torture. All part of the madness and upheaval that ran through the twentieth century like so many lines of bloody dominoes, sparked by two shots from Gavrilo Princip's Browning Model 1910 in a side street off Sarajevo's Appel Quay. And my life, woven all through it like a scarlet thread....

And where was I in 1942, when they shot the Hangman of Prague, when they held out against the SS here? Tracking down an ex-Black Eagle who'd joined the French Resistance. They were killing Nazis and I'd been getting ready to kill someone who fought them, all to avenge a dead Empire, for a cause no longer worthwhile if it ever had been to start with.

So easy to commit to the wrong cause and waste a life in its service; at least I had the advantage of having additional lifetimes in which to redeem my errors, assuming that's possible. I sit in one of the cathedral pews and clasp my hands before my mouth, but have no idea what I should say. I hope to feel some presence around or above me, but there's nothing. Perhaps there's nothing to feel, or perhaps it's simply denied me. I'm starting to annoy myself, asking such unanswerable questions again and again.

Vienna. I want to move on, to Vienna; see my former capital at close quarters once again. *Einspänner* and *Linzer torte*, as I promised myself. But first, I've another, long-delayed visit to pay.

I hire a car; I've had enough of public transport for now. Driving myself at least gives me an illusion of control. I take the E65 out of Prague and head south-east, taking the D1 highway through Central Bohemia into Vysočina. 'Vysočina' literally means 'the Highlands', and that's what you get: it's the most sparsely-populated part of Czechia and its quiet vistas of peaks, fields and woodlands bring me much-needed calm and peace.

Which is more than can be said for the highway itself. Construction started on the D1 almost a century ago, and having been interrupted by the Second World War, Stalinism and other minor inconveniences, the two-lane road just can't cope with twenty-first century traffic. It suffers from constant tailbacks, while the roadworks intended to modernise the highway only make the congestion worse. *Everyone* hates the D1.

Unfortunately I only find this out after several hours on the blasted thing. At least the scenery's nice, but given the amount of time I have to spend gazing at it, the charm wears thin. I follow the highway into South Moravia and make an overnight stop in Brno

– even if I hadn't been considering doing so anyway, I can't face another hour on the D1.

In the hotel, my fingers hover over the laptop's keyboard; so easy to type the Czech or German version of the name I'm looking for into a search engine, but I don't. I'll wait to be surprised.

The following afternoon finds me on Route 53, heading towards Znojmo, high on the rocks above the Thaya River, and the edge of the Podyji National Park. But I turn away from the walled hilltop town – another day, perhaps – leave the main roads, and set off in search of Bradenstein.

———

It isn't even called Bradenstein anymore, but I knew that from my last visit, back in 1932. Kamenice-Brada, they call it now, although I'm surprised it's called anything at all; when I last saw my childhood home it was a long-abandoned ruin. The only sign for it then had been a battered, crudely-lettered one saying BRADA KÁMEN, which isn't even good Czech – probably the work of some long-ago panicked Imperial functionary with a poor command of the language trying to curry favour as things fell apart in '18.

It would already have been empty then, Papa having shot himself earlier that year. My fault, that – well, mine and Ulrich's. We were listed as dead after we walked the Gate: the last of his five children, all fed into the War's greedy mouth, or so it seemed; with Mama gone as well, he saw no reason to carry on.

And that was before the Second War; before the Russians, too. What chance would such a place have of survival? And yet road signs point the way to Kamenice-Brada. I don't know what I expect to find when I take the half-familiar road leading to the estate. An even more rotted, decaying shell? Rubble almost lost beneath the grass? Or all trace of it scrubbed away, replaced with a housing estate or factory?

The first shock is the gatehouse: when I turn the final corner, it's in front of me, as it always used to be when I was little. In 1932 the wrought-iron gates were long-gone, most likely filched by some enterprising thief for the scrap value. Broken windows, missing doors, the stonework cracked and pitted from hammer-blows.

But now, the gates are back. They're black-painted wrought-iron, topped with gold-painted spikes, and there's a very familiar family crest in the centre of each. The stonework's been cleaned and restored; there are new windows and a polished, gleaming door. The gates stand open, thankfully: if I had to explain myself to a keeper I'd be too tongue-tied to speak. I drive through.

Beyond the gate, the road slopes down. The house gleams in the evening twilight: clean ivory-white, chased with gold. The lawns are neatly trimmed, the grounds and woods landscaped once again.

The lake glitters as I approach the house, but I don't look. Too many memories. I rescued Ulrich when he fell through the ice there: if I hadn't, would I be here now? I couldn't follow him into the *Falkenjaeger* if he wasn't alive to join them.

The newly tarmacked road gives way to a gravelled forecourt; I park there.

Someone's clearly bought the old place and restored it, for whatever reason; someone with taste as well as money, or at least enough money to buy its appearance. Some wealthy robber-baron, maybe, aping the nobility of old.

The old gravel paths snake through the lawns; I follow one to an ornamental fountain I always loved. She's still there, twined around the central spout: a beautiful mermaid with bare, perfect breasts. My first love, when I was little. My first real love was my maid, Katrin, and remembering her makes me turn to the lake at last. Crying in her arms after rescuing Ulrich, my head on her soft, soft breasts...

Other lives, other loves, other days.

It's quiet. Hushed. There's a distant plop from the lake as a fish jumps. And for the first time since I lost you, I feel something close to peace. Like coming home. But then, I *am* home. And yet, I'm not.

"Beautiful, isn't it?"

I didn't even hear him approach. I spin, hand going to the Roth-Steyr. But then I see his face and freeze, open-mouthed.

The man steps back, hands raised. "Sorry. Didn't mean to—" Then his mouth opens too. "Good Lord."

He's speaking English, with the faintest of Northern accents.

He's also my brother Conrad, who died in the Italian Alps in 1918.

———— ~ ————

We stand in the entrance hall, looking at the portraits. My brothers: Ulrich, Rolf and Franz. Conrad too, of course. Mama and Papa.

And me.

Papa commissioned them in 1913, with the war a year away. The Balkan Wars, which at the time we'd feared would spark that wider conflict, had just ended: the Bulgarians, Greeks, Serbs and Montenegrins had first seized territory from the Turks, then fought over the spoils. It had been the lull before the storm: we all knew a bigger war was coming, though we couldn't have guessed its appalling magnitude, or how thoroughly it would destroy the world we knew.

I remember sitting for the painter in the August heat as he fussed, first over his sketchbook, then his easel, trying to capture my likeness. He managed well enough, in the end: enough that, despite my glasses and shaven head, my host recognised me.

"Don't know what it is," he says. "Same old faces keep cropping up, generation after generation. Must be the inbreeding, I suppose." He smiles to show it's a joke.

I shrug. "Far as I know, I'm no relation. Who knows, though? If you go far enough back…" I give my English a German accent; I've told him I'm a tourist from Düsseldorf. "When did you find out?"

"Only recently. They kept his background quiet, I suppose. Growing up in the War, and after it, in Britain – they wouldn't have wanted to advertise being part-German."

Part-Austrian, but who'd have cared about such distinctions? "You knew him?"

"Not well. I was only very little when I died. But yes, although as I say, no one discussed his background. I just knew he'd come over to get away from Hitler."

History, it seems, still has surprises for me. After a century believing I was the last Bradenstein-Vršovci, it turns out I'm not.

Franz and Conrad were both listed as killed in the 'White War' between Habsburg and Italian forces in the Alps: Franz in the failed Asiago counteroffensive in May 1916, Conrad at the First Battle of Monte Grappa, in the autumn of 1917. Conrad, however, had been misidentified as another soldier who'd been killed beside him, and the dead man misidentified as Conrad. He'd spent months alternately comatose, drugged or delirious: by the time the Army – then in disarray and crumbling as defeat approached – realised its error and remembered to inform the family, Ulrich and I were also 'dead'. Worse, so was Mama, which ensured the news my father still had one living child reached him too late.

Conrad – this other, present-day Conrad; he's called Conrad too, named for his great-grandfather – tells me how after the estate was seized by the new Czechoslovak government – another union that dissolved in my lifetime – my brother returned to Vienna. Our family were always as much Moravian as Austrian, but Europe between the wars was a place of sharply-defined, either-or allegiances as the new nations born from the collapse of empires defined their borders and identities through revolution, counter-revolution and ethnic cleansing. Having the wrong name on the wrong side of a border could be a dangerous affair, not least because where those borders lay was often defined by the race of those within them…

So Conrad had gone to Austria, trying to find a place in a nation reduced to a tiny, landlocked vestige of its Imperial grandeur. Many ex-soldiers fell in with the right-wing paramilitaries that swelled the Nazis' ranks in years to come, but Conrad's experiences had made all war's trappings abhorrent to him. He became a leftist – a democratic socialist, no less! Perhaps for the best that Papa shot himself; else he'd have given himself a stroke…

Conrad Bradenstein, as he was then known – no titles in the new Austria, and a Czech-sounding name like 'Vršovci' would only have complicated matters – was a pacifist for a time, but reluctantly renounced that stance after the brief but vicious Civil War of 1934. The right-wing Fatherland Front brutally repressed the Social Democrats and ushered in what became known as Austrofascism. Conrad was arrested, but friends procured his release and he left Austria for the last time – first for France, then England when the Nazis invaded in 1940. And in Britain he met his wife, the present-day Conrad's great-grandmother. He married her, Anglicised his name to Bradstone, and, much to everyone's surprise, started a family in his forties.

"They'd told him he'd be lucky to last another ten years, apparently," Young Conrad says. "After he was wounded in Italy, I mean. More like five, they reckoned, and he could forget about kids."

"I'm guessing he proved them wrong, then."

He laughs. "Very much so. My Mum always said it's a pity they couldn't bottle whatever he had. He lived to ninety-seven and had three children. Plus plenty of grandkids and…" Young Conrad gestures to himself "…great-grandkids."

I chuckle. It's a strange, but good, story to hear. I think so, anyway. I've thought of myself as the last of my family for so long – other than Ulrich, anyway. And all that time, in England. I might have passed them in the street, the Brandenstein diaspora, and never known them. Would I have even known Conrad, after the changes war and time had wreaked?

If I'd known, I could have been part of their lives, at least for a time. And Ulrich? If he'd known, could I have peeled him away from the *Falkenjaeger*, his blind devotion to a dead cause?

If I had, if I only had – what then? The others, like Erick and Tibor: without Ulrich, would they have given up too? The thought of it. I would have known my family. I wouldn't have had to kill my brother.

And you would still be alive.

The waste of it. The sheer fucking waste.

"Are you all right?" Conrad asks; I realise, to my horror, I'm crying. Quickly I turn away.

"Sorry, is there a bathroom? I just need to—"

"Just through there."

It's a new one; they had them at Bradenstein in my day, but time's marched on since then. I shut the door behind me, grip the sink's edges and take deep breaths. It's all clamouring for release within me: the shock and turmoil, the grief and the pointlessness, the fucking *futility* of it all. I could bawl right now, like a little child. But I don't. Mustn't. He can't know. I take deep breaths and force the tears down instead, promising them they can come out later, like a mother pacifying unruly children – like the ones I never had a chance to know, the nieces and nephews and… no, I can't think of that. I'll fall apart.

I pull up my sleeve and bite my wrist till I taste blood. Give the pain somewhere to go. Wrap a handkerchief round the bite to staunch it, then pull the sleeve back down so it's concealed. Splash cold water into my face. Towel it dry. Then a deep breath, and go out to meet my great-great nephew.

The gardens of Bradenstein, at dusk; we sit on a terrace, sipping coffee. Just like old times.

Young Conrad's glad of the company: people work on the estate during the week, of course, but not today. His friends, his business partners, are all in Prague or Berlin. He's far from home and family. Friendships spring up quickly and easily at times like this.

There's a summerhouse beside the lake, a favourite place of mine, overlooking a miniature marsh of bulrushes that open out into the wide, glassy expanse of water. I loved sitting there at dawn, watching the sun come up, the mist drifting through the reeds. I went there after I heard about Conrad; lay exhausted and cried-out on a couch, my head in Tibor's lap.

Tibor was home on leave, convalescing from an illness. He did his best for me, but his spirits were low as well: he'd known and liked Conrad, even been rather smitten with him at one time. He stayed silent in the end, stroking my hair. And the mist dispersed and the sun came up, and it was another day and my brothers were dead.

First Franz had died, then Rolf. Rolf was always the one who had to be different. (Of the boys, at least – if there was ever a black sheep I thought it was me.) Conrad, Franz and Ulrich joined the Army, so of course Rolf joined the Navy instead. He loved the water: forever swimming, or boating. Ulrich and I once sailed to the island in the middle of the lake to declare our own kingdom, but we got the idea from Rolf's visits there.

Maybe best he died: no Navy, after all, in Austria or even Czechoslovakia after the war. I don't mean that, of course. It wasn't better. He ended up commanding a U-boat: I don't know how close being sealed in a steel cigar beneath the surface came to whatever he'd dreamed of.

Rolf was the quietest of us: separate, apart somehow. He had secrets, I think, the rest of us were never privy to. Of all my brothers, I knew him least. It's one of my great regrets.

Anyway: in 1917, a few months before Conrad's death was reported, Rolf's ship was lost with all hands. We never found out what happened. The best guess was that they'd hit a mine, but no one knew for sure; no wreckage or bodies were ever recovered. They just went to sea one day, and never returned.

Even then, I'd wanted to know him better; I was somehow sure the two of us might have much in common, if he'd only open up. But that chance was now gone.

Franz, then Rolf, then Conrad, and only two of us were left: Ulrich and I. Papa was like stone, an old-school soldier who'd sooner break in pieces than shed a tear, but we could see the damage: his hair greyed and he grew thinner, stooped, the lines of his craggy face deepening. Painful to watch though that was, with Mama it was worse.

Losing three sons in two years hit her like bullets; she wept and faded. I remember she fell very ill after Rolf died: shouts in the night, a doctor summoned quickly. I was too wrapped-up in my own grief, and the drinking and sex I tried to numb it with, to realise until many years later she'd tried to kill herself that night. After Conrad died, Papa often slept during the day, sitting up at night to watch over her. So much I understood only in retrospect.

After Conrad, though, my grief gave way to anger. I'd had enough. It wasn't really patriotism, or even revenge: I just wanted it all to stop, while something was still left. So I used every connection I had, and began working for the *Evidenzbüro*. Short of dressing as a man and joining the Army – which some women did, and I briefly considered – it was the only fighting I could do.

But the War was lost and everything ended. Then, with Mama slowly dying and Papa a shell of himself, Ulrich told me about the *Falkenjaeger* and how he'd been chosen for them, and I persuaded them to use me too...

Sometimes I think the weight of all I've lost will pull me under, and I don't know how to fight it – if I can, or even should. The lovers I've had over the years helped anchor me, but you were the one I loved deepest. And now you're gone.

Young Conrad tells me how Bradenstein – Kamenice-Brada – changed hands over the years, somehow always escaping demolition, till a Czech-German company bought the estate two years ago, to convert it into a hotel resort and spa. Young Conrad's an architect with a background in restoring classic buildings; with his family connection to the place, they couldn't sign him up quickly enough.

A hotel. Papa would have bellowed for his shotgun at the idea, and Mama would have swooned. Franz would have stormed and shouted; Ulrich would have been outraged, too, but coldly so, already plotting how to foil so dastardly a scheme. Conrad, always patient and fatalistic, would have sighed and shrugged. And Rolf? I honestly don't know what Rolf would have said, or done. My brother the enigma, even in death.

I can picture Tibor's reaction, though; see his head thrown back in laughter at the absurdity of it all, the great joke. Me? I'm just glad to see the place as I remember it once again. Better a hotel than a ruin. I could come here again; I could stay. I could deceive myself, if only briefly, that I was home.

But not with you. In another life, I've told you everything; we stayed together and came here. And Tibor left the *Falkenjaeger* and joined us, and the three of us will sit out by the summerhouse some fine dawn and watch the mist in the reeds. In another life. But not in this.

I've got to stop thinking like that, or I'll cry again. I should talk about something. Anything. "How did you restore the portraits?" I ask Young Conrad.

"Oh, they didn't need restoring, just buying. The artist was a Czech – bit of a hero of the independence movement – so after the Empire broke up his paintings were all snapped up by various galleries and private collections. The Bradenstein-Vršovci ones aren't considered his best or most important, though, so…"

He trails off. Perhaps he's realised my attention's wandered from him, that I'm not listening any longer, or perhaps he's heard what I have.

Engines.

I look up towards the gatehouse road, and see the first pair of headlights coming down the hill.

Then a second.

Then a third.

Three cars. People carriers. All in uniform black.

"Who's this?" Young Conrad murmurs. No fear, only curiosity. I both pity and envy him, and feel the protective urge you'd feel for a child about to wander into traffic.

I've just found what's left of my family, and now I'm about to lose it again, if whoever's in these cars has their way. They won't want any witnesses. I know, with cold and deadly certainty, that Berlin has followed me here.

"Trouble, I'm afraid." I take off the glasses – they'll only get in the way – and stuff the headscarf in a pocket; I might find a use for it. I take out the Roth-Steyr and pull back the bolt. Young Conrad's eyes go round. "Get back inside the house. Lock the doors."

"What?" he stares. "What's happening?"

"I'm very sorry." The cars are halfway down the road. "Thought I'd dealt with this. They're after me, but if you get in the way…"

"I'll call the police," he says: an offer, not a threat.

"It'll all be over before they get here," I say gently. "Get inside. Lock the doors." He's so like Conrad. But so much younger to look at. And so very innocent. And enough innocents have died for me. "I'll keep you safe," I promise.

He runs for the house and I watch the cars come; when the door we came through slams and locks, I move.

If I die today, I die. But so will these. I'll protect what's left of my family, come what may.

The most important thing is to lead them away from the house and Young Conrad. But they know I'm not alone, and there's more than enough of them to split the group in two, half chasing me and half storming the house. If that happens, Young Conrad won't stand a chance.

I have to hit them hard on arrival, when they're bunched together. Kill as many as I can, leave them too depleted to divide their forces, then fall back; make them send their full remaining strength after me.

Besides, I only have a pistol: to begin with, at least, it'll be close work. But I can do that.

Three cars, each holding up to seven: call it twenty-one. Bad odds, but I've faced worse. Although usually with the goal of punching through them, rather than wiping them out. And they usually didn't have anything that could kill me.

But things change.

Bad odds, but I've one advantage: this is my home. Young Conrad's restoration is near-perfect: I know the terrain.

I'm waiting, tucked behind a statue at the edge of the drive, when the cars come hissing into the forecourt, doors opening as they halt. Men in black jumpsuits emerge: black-suited women, too. Whoever my enemy is, he's an equal-opportunity employer. They form three groups, one making for the main door, the others moving to encircle the building.

Three squads of six. One blacksuit stays with each car. Each carries a Steyr AUG assault rifle, an automatic pistol in a hip holster, and a boot-sheathed knife.

But I'm ready, and as they move so do I: low, quick and silent, across the gravel, to the nearest blacksuit.

She turns at the last second, raising her gun; I fling gravel in her eyes and kick her under the knee. When she goes down my scarf's looped around her neck and pulled tight, choking off her scream. Twist and pull, and her neck snaps. I let her drop and take her rifle, firing a zig-zag burst after one of the flanking groups as they run for the lake terrace. Mostly chest and head shots: four go down and are still; another writhes and screams. The last one bolts for cover.

Then I spin and roll as the other blacksuits open fire, pulverising the car. I empty the AUG in reply, dropping one of the remaining drivers and three of the squad making for the front door.

Move.

I ditch the rifle and take the dead girl's pistol: a Steyr M9. Whoever my enemies are, they love the Steyr company's weapons: the same firm that made sidearms for the Imperial Army. Including my own gun.

I weave for the lake terrace, gunfire chasing me all the way. The wounded man's now dead, but I tuck and roll as the last of the squad fires a burst from some bushes. I put five rounds into his cover and he staggers out, firing wild. I drop him with a headshot.

I empty the M9 towards the car park, toss it aside and take another dead man's guns. And then I run again.

Counting the dead:

All six of the first group. Three of the second. Two drivers.

Eleven men and women, in less than a minute.

That leaves ten. All coming after me, as I'd hoped.

I fall back towards the lake by stages. There's a tree here, a statue there, a wall somewhere else; I use each for shelter, then as the blacksuits close in, open fire with the AUG. I get two of them the first time, from behind the tree.

Eight left.

The second time I pull that trick – from behind the statue – they're too fast and all find cover in time. But on the third attempt, when I reach the wall, my luck's with me again and I kill two more. The others find cover and fire back; one raises his head just a little too high. I squeeze the rifle's trigger. One shot: *crack*.

And then there were five.

A moment's silence. The sulphur smell of gunsmoke taints the air. Other smells too: blood, shit, bodies opened up.

I check the AUG's magazine. Four rounds left. But I still have an M9 – and the Roth-Steyr.

I hear the cogs turning in the survivors' brains as they do the calculations: less than a quarter of them left, and not a scratch on me.

Turn tail. Head home. That would be the easiest way. But I don't know if they'll dare.

It's worth trying.

"If you stop now, you can live," I call out, in German. "Just turn around and go. Nobody else has to die today."

I feel the air shift, and know I've said the wrong thing. A moment ago, I seemed invincible; now they think I'm afraid, maybe even wounded.

Till now they've reacted, not acted. I struck and fell back; they followed because they wanted me dead. Now I've let them stop and think. Given them a chance to plan.

I move to fire over the wall, glimpse a muzzle flash and duck. A bullet fractures stone, inches above my head. I drop, move over to my right and come up to fire again; this time I feel the bullet brush my scalp. Each one's watching a different section of wall, waiting for me to pop up.

Stupid. Stupid. This is war. *Geheimerkreig*. No place for laws, for the *code duello* or Geneva Convention. They won't retreat. If I want to live – if I want Young Conrad to live – they have to die.

And now I've given them the initiative.

Through a gap in the top of the wall I see them spreading out, making harder targets of themselves. Two blacksuits break cover, weaving back towards the house. For a split-second I actually think I've panicked them, but then duck down again as the others lay down covering fire, shattering more stone above my head.

They're going after Young Conrad, and there's only one of me: I can't go after the runners and the shooters at the same time.

The gunfire changes. Three automatic weapons were firing: now there's only one. Short, tight bursts hitting the brick and concrete overhead. I stay low, crouching. Hold the AUG one-handed; heft the M9 in my left. Wait for their move. Try not to think about the runners weaving towards the house, about Young Conrad alone inside, lost and afraid, caught up in a war begun decades before his birth. Another innocent, like Hanna.

I can't protect him if I'm dead. Two blacksuits are going for the house. Only one weapon's firing at me, which means it must be covering the last two blacksuits as they close in on my position.

I go still, eyes shut, listening. I know what they'll do. What I'd do. Ulrich, Albin, Erick, Stefan or Mathias would lay down fire to keep the quarry's head down; Tibor and I would move to opposite ends of the wall, fire round the sides and catch the target in a crossfire.

I listen; listen…

A muffled clink of metal, very close.

Wait.

Ready.

And…

A flicker of black in my peripheral vision, to my right: I throw myself backwards, arms outflung. The earth where I crouched explodes. I fire the assault rifle, blowing out those last four rounds. I'm aiming for the chest but they go high: the right-hand blacksuit's face explodes. At the same time I'm pumping the M9's trigger too, but I was never a great left-handed shot and I'm not looking at the target. A line of bullets tears across the grass towards me. I roll, over and over, firing two-handed now: the second blacksuit stands a-jittering until the magazine empties. Without the bullets holding him up, he tumbles to the ground.

I run to the first blacksuit, reload the M9, take his AUG. People keep giving me these, I think, trying not to laugh.

Three left. Two closing on the house, if not already there; one tucked in a hollow in the ground, rifle shouldered, waiting for me to show my face.

I cleared out of Berlin, but someone's still coming after me; someone still wants me dead. I need to know who; I'd take one of these alive, if I could, but I know they won't give me the option.

So I'll have to kill them, and fast, before Young Conrad's hurt. The only problem is that I can't pop my head up without my friend in the hollow shooting it off.

So I break cover and run at him.

The assault rifle's muzzle flashes. I weave, firing both the pistol and my own rifle. Something whips by my ear; something slams into my left arm. The pistol flies away.

I hit the ground and the man in the hollow makes his first and last mistake: he stands up to finish me off. When he does, I pull my rifle's trigger and cut him in half.

I drag myself to his side, pull my numb, wounded arm in front of me and prop the Steyr on it, stock tucked into my shoulder. The last two blacksuits are on either side of the French windows, since for all they know Young Conrad's holed up inside with a Kalashnikov. One aims his rifle at the doors; the other raises hers as a club to smash the glass.

The man goes still, realising the shooting's stopped; he turns and brings his gun around.

A three-round burst, dead-centre in the chest, slams him back against the wall.

The woman fires wildly, running for cover. I fire back; she spins and pitches through the French windows, whirling and falling headlong, in a blizzard of glass.

The man drops his gun and falls to his knees. His expression is somewhere between perplexity and that of a child afraid of the dark. Then he falls forward; I hear his skull crack against the stone, the gristly pop as his nose breaks. I let go of the AUG and roll onto my back, groaning at the pain in my arm. Silence rushes back in over Bradenstein, and after a moment there's distant splash as a fish jumps in the lake.

The bullet slashed across my upper arm: a gouge, nothing more. In the half-hour since the gunfight, an ordinary bullet wound would have healed, but this one will take as long as any injury to an ordinary woman. Still: a few inches to the right and I'd be dead, so this is preferable.

Young Conrad's dressed the wound. He's very pale and still shaking, but other than that he's coping well.

Silence reigns supreme. No police sirens or blue lights: I talked Young Conrad out of that, at least for now, and the place is too distant for anyone else to have heard the gunfire.

Convincing Young Conrad made for some additional inconvenience, but not much, and it'll be gone soon enough. The remains of my left thumb are on the kitchen chopping block, beside the cleaver I used and a few drops of blood. As always, the severed body part's disintegrating rapidly, already resembling the tube of ash from a burned-out cigarette. A touch, and it'll fall apart. I'd best make sure it's disposed of, and the board and cleaver cleaned, before I go.

The new thumb's almost fully regrown. The more traumatic the wound – when made by an ordinary weapon – the quicker it heals. By the time I go, there won't even be a scar.

I pour us a large brandy each. Not medically recommended, I'm sure, but it takes my mind off the ache in my arm. And helps Young Conrad get over the double shock of having a minor war break out in his new back garden, and hearing my little tale.

The story I so long wanted to tell you; that I whispered in your ear when you were dead. Despite my earlier intention to keep him in blissful ignorance, I've told Young Conrad everything. I have to remind myself, telling it, that I'm not talking to you. It's a lot to take in, never mind believe. Hence the thumb-

and-cleaver routine: a picture (or, in this case, live demonstration) is worth a thousand words, and so forth.

When I'm done, neither of us speaks. What do you say in these circumstances, after all? The Viennese society I grew up in was big on etiquette and protocol, but even they wouldn't have had anything to cover this. I start to worry I've hit him with too much all at once, and that he'll end up rocking back and forth under the table mumbling 'whibble whibble whibble' and sucking his thumb.

"I'm sorry," I tell him at last. "I've brought all this down on you, and… if I'd known, I'd never have come."

"You wouldn't?" he looks at me. "Never?"

"Not with this lot after me, I mean. I honestly thought once I was out of Berlin, they'd leave me alone."

"So if you'd known you still had a family?"

I realise, contemplating the question, that I never even bothered to carry out so much as the most cursory research, even when the internet made it so much simpler and easier to do. Didn't even type the family name into a search engine: hadn't had even a moment's curiosity what history – official history, the only kind most people know – says of the house of Bradenstein-Vršovci. How, and if, its last generation is remembered: Ulrich and I, Rolf and Franz and Conrad. Five minutes on Google, and I might have known about Conrad years ago. What *would* I have done then? Most likely – especially if I'd been with you – I'd have left that stone unturned. It would've been a complication I didn't need.

Unless, of course, I'd thought to tell you everything. Reveal who I truly was. Knowing about the Bradstones might have even pushed me to tell you all. For a moment, again, I imagine a different world.

In another life.

"Maybe," I tell him. "If I'd thought it was safe."

Or not. My last century of existence has been a succession of lies, after all – false names, false identities, false lives I could flit away from whenever they became inconvenient. But the world's shrunk since I left the others: it's filled with new technologies that make it harder to slip through the cracks. Not impossible, though – I'd better hope not, anyway. For three-quarters of a century, until a few short months ago, I lived quietly and within the law. None of my past identities had to bear the level of scrutiny that'll be brought to bear now.

Even so, I always travelled light: emotionally speaking, you were the most I wanted to carry. Having a family again might have left me feeling trapped.

"So," says Young Conrad, "what now?"

A good question: I'm not sure if he forgot to ask before or just assumed I had a plan.

"I'll tie you up before I leave," I say. "That way you're still the innocent bystander."

"What about you?" There's genuine concern on his face, bless him. I don't know how he's got anywhere in business: he's like a lamb.

"Well, first of all I've some dead bodies to search."

He grimaces. "What for?"

"Because *I've* been reacting instead of acting too, and that needs to change."

He doesn't get it, but that doesn't matter.

I don't expect to find anything on the dead blacksuits, and I don't. No ID, nor anything to suggest who sent them. Unsurprising, but annoying.

I wear latex gloves for the search; I've wiped down every surface I remember touching, especially the guns. I'd be astonished if Okelo and Trautmann haven't linked me to the dead hitmen in Berlin, especially as one was almost certainly carrying the machine-pistol that shot Hanna. And while I didn't leave any fingerprints there, they'll be all over the Charlottenburg apartment – and how long before they're linked with those of Valerie Varden, the missing mortuary technician from Manchester? I can change my name, even my appearance up to a point, but not my fingerprints.

The smartest move's to run to another continent; lose myself there for a few years – or decades – until the trail's cold. Plenty of warzones and plague zones where bullets, bombs, disease or poison gas would pose no threat, where I could disappear and still do a hell of a lot of good, if that's what I still want.

And, much as I'd enjoy a quiet life again, that does have a certain appeal. But first there's the matter of the blacksuits, and the hitmen in Berlin. Would I have found anything if I'd searched them? Too late to think of it now.

I search the cars, again not expecting much. There's nothing in the first one. I search the second vehicle but find nothing there either. The last vehicle seems just as bare, till I have one last grope around the empty glove compartment and find a scrap of crumpled pasteboard: a business card, the same deep shiny beetle-black as the cars themselves.

Highly quality card and production values; simple, unflashy design. A name, a website and an email address in plain white lettering. Not even a phone number. In the centre there's a compass rose like the NATO logo, only in black and white. But what stands out is the name:

VIRIBUS UNITIS SICHERHEIT GmBH
WIEN

Viribus Unitis. Meaning *With United Forces.* When the Great War broke out, the *SMS Viribus Unitis* was the Austro-Hungarian flagship. An unusual name chosen because – more importantly – it was the Emperor's personal motto.

No way *that's* a coincidence.

I consider asking Young Conrad if he's got round to installing wi-fi at Bradenstein yet – I could do a little research before I leave – but it's better not to take the risk, and be on my way. I go back into the house, find some rope and tie him to a suitably stout chair.

"Um," he says. "How long will I be—"

"I'll tip the police off. Don't worry."

"Will I be seeing you again?"

He looks so like Conrad, yet so unlike. Boyish, innocent – sweet – in a way my generation never had the chance to be.

"Possibly," I say. "But I doubt it. Take care of yourself."

"You too."

And with that, I turn my back on the family I didn't even know existed till only hours before.

Outside, I take one last look at the old place, trying not to see the bodies on the lawns and forecourt. Bradenstein. My home, and yet not my home, again.

The hire-car's somehow escaped any major damage. One window's shattered, but I just wind down what's left of it: it's a warm night, and promises to be a fine day tomorrow. In the dark, it'll go unnoticed; by morning, I'll have left it and Czechia behind me, on my way to Vienna.

After all these years, I'm finally going back.

———

I drive south till I find a motorway services. Among the items I picked up in Prague are a handful of burner phones: true to my word, I ring the police, tip them off about Bradenstein, then slip the phone into the back of a passing pickup truck. Once I'm over the border I ditch the car, then hitch-hike to Retz and catch the train.

By the time I reach Vienna, nearly an hour and a half later, my looks have changed again: my hair was already growing back, so I shaved it at the sides only, giving myself a flat-top, and dyed it black. Now I'm back in jeans and boots, with a plain t-shirt and plain black leather jacket. Just another butch, looking for her femme.

So many places I haven't seen in so long – the Hofburg, Schönbrunn Palace, the Staatsoper, the Riesenrad looming high above the Prater, all with their own memories both sweet and bitter – but there's only one place I want to go now. Something I promised both of us, before I knew you were dead.

On a street in Vienna's Old Town called the Herrengasse stands the Café Central. Inside, ivory pillars hold up vaulted ceilings: chandeliers and arched windows let the light in to gleam off the polished floor. Square, good-sized tables with crisp white cloths. I order *Einspänner* coffee and *Linzer torte*; both are delicious. I order a second coffee.

Tibor and I would come here to revitalise ourselves after a heavy night out. You could spend all day here, reading, writing or sketching. Our favourite was Leon Trotsky's old haunt, the Griensteidl, but that closed a few years ago. He used to come here as well, though. As did Sigmund Freud, Stefan Zweig and Robert Musil. And both Hitler and Stalin. I wonder if they ever all sat here at the same time, dreaming their different dreams and nightmares, planning their masterworks, theories and futures. I remember wanting to come here with you. I wish both that you were here now, and that I hadn't come: your absence is a physical ache, my grief at losing you hitting me harder than at any time since your death. It's all I can do not to begin sobbing, but somehow I manage to finish the second *Einspänner*, then pay the bill and go.

I walk quickly up Herrengasse to the Radisson Blu, where I'm staying. In my room, I let myself cry. Then I shower and rest – though with the Roth-Steyr close at hand – before finally powering up the cheap laptop I bought in Prague, connecting to the hotel's wi-fi and beginning my search.

There's very little online about Viribus Unitis Security, other than what I'd already guessed. You won't find their people guarding car parks or building sites: they provide consultants and bodyguards to blue-chip clients, and reading between the lines I suspect they're involved in shadier operations too, at home and overseas. The website doesn't have an address for their offices, but I find that with a little online sleuthing. Not much else, though.

There's really only one way I'm going to dig up further information all by myself, and that's by visiting their offices. Not that I'm going in daylight hours: they might let me in, but I'm unlikely to walk back out.

I consider breaking in; it wouldn't be my first time, although it *would* be the first in several decades (last time was in the early '90s, at the behest of that left-wing group I mentioned earlier;) I wish I'd kept all my less socially acceptable skills sharp in the interim. I make a mental note to do so if I actually survive all this: some have definitely rusted, and if the last few months have taught me anything, it's that my past isn't going to leave me alone.

I sit back on the bed, studying the card. Are Viribus Unitis remnants of the Black Eagles, or the *Falkenjaeger*? The name could suggest either group since both were, in their different ways, about carrying on the Empire's legacy, although I'm leaning more towards the Black Eagles: they were supposed to recreate it, the *Falkenjaeger* only to avenge it.

Having found their head office on Google Maps I do my best to survey it, but most of it's greyed out. I wish I'd taken a few of the blacksuits' guns when I left Bradenstein. A Steyr AUG would even the odds considerably, not to mention one or two M9 automatics with their magazines that hold eighteen rounds against the Roth-Steyr's ten and which are far quicker to load. Even if I did, though, I'd be outnumbered and outgunned if I broke in and – unlike at Bradenstein – this time they'd have the home ground advantage.

I don't *want* to break in anyway, if I can avoid it. I *could* do it, but I was never any kind of genius at it.

That time in the '90s, we were nearly caught a dozen times and only weren't because of sheer luck. And as for the time before…

Actually, I have to smile when I think of that. It was pretty much the one occasion during our 1925 visit to Berlin that Tibor and I attempted something to do with our mission, rather than just getting hammered and fucking every willing partner in sight.

Back then, the Nazis existed, but were still new and only one of many paramilitary gangs who wanted to bring back the Kaiser, or another dictatorial strongman, hang the Jews and Communists and probably shoot all the queers as well. (Although not necessarily all, at least to begin with: while there were gay men and women who fought the Nazis and suffered for it, in later years some of Weimar's more prominent dykes, like Ruth Roellig and Selli Engler, collaborated with the fuckers, to say nothing of all the leading brownshirts who were raging queens.) There were any number of strutting dickheads looking for a brawl or a putsch, whichever seemed more likely, and it had occurred to us both that ex-Black Eagles might feel at home among them. Even if it wasn't Austria-Hungary, they'd still have loved the idea of a new Germanic Imperium in Central Europe.

There was a rumour that one particular Black Eagle was active in a small but vicious far-right party called the FDP, or Für Deutschland Partei. He looked the Aryan dream and spoke perfect German, but was in fact Hungarian: a former Honvéd officer called Tasziló Czobor.

Czobor *was*, in fact, a part of the group in question, and his files would have been in their cabinets when we broke into their offices that night: he later joined the NSDAP (having seen where the far-right wind was blowing,) became a high-ranking SS officer and was the last Black Eagle I killed in the *Geheimkrieg*. That was in Berlin, but not in '25: it was two decades later, as the Russians smashed their way into the city.

And why was that? Well…

Reason number one: the slivovitz. Slivovitz is a plum brandy found all over Central and Eastern Europe: you can use it to run farm machinery, remove barnacles from boat hulls, or, in extreme situations, you can drink it. Tibor got us a bottle each, and I think it was about seventy-five percent pure alcohol: if we hadn't walked the Sindelar Gate it would have probably killed us. As it was, it's safe to say it may have impaired our judgement.

Reason number two: the cocaine. Under other circumstances we might still have had the sense to postpone the break-in till another night, but I'd laid hands on a substantial amount of coke from a friend. And as anyone who's ever snorted enough Bolivian marching powder will testify, one very common side effect's a ridiculous amount of overconfidence. And so, simultaneously weaving drunk and bouncing up and down with nervous energy, me with one eye twitching insanely and Tibor with a non-stop nosebleed that dripped a trail wherever we went, we broke into the party's offices to ransack the filing cabinets.

Even then, we might have got away with it. Might have had Czobor's details, or even Czobor himself, to show for our Berlin stopover by the time Ulrich and the rest came back a fortnight later, rather than an apartment that resembled a pig-sty and an assortment of confused and hungover lovers who were rapidly shooed out the door.

Unfortunately, there was a third factor:

The dogs.

The FDP's leader, a charming little sadist called Hansi Kleiger, owned several gigantic hunting dogs. I've no idea *what* they'd been bred to hunt (Tibor suggested dragons,) but they were devoted to him, tolerated his followers and were near-homicidal towards anyone else. We already knew that, having often seen Kleiger and two of his most strapping thugs being dragged around Berlin by the beasts. What we didn't know, until we found out the hard way, was that he locked his dogs in the FDP's offices overnight, every night.

The worst part was they were cunning, not making a sound when we clumsily forced the lock and blundered into the offices, but padding silently to investigate. We were trying to force a filing cabinet open when we heard the first growl and turned to see three of the monsters trying to push their way through the office door at once; it looked like we were about to be attacked by Cerberus.

"Nice doggy," Tibor whispered. "Who's a good boy?" To which the only response was another, considerably more seismic, growl. I could think of nothing to say or do, other than wish we'd stayed at home to finish off the cocaine.

"Oh, shit," said Tibor, and the dogs ran at us.

We were both armed, but they were fast and it was dark. Plus, if I'm honest, I'd have struggled to shoot another dog, even one of Kleiger's. Horváth had made me kill a little terrier as final proof of my commitment at the end of my *Falkenjaeger* training, and I still regretted it. Still do. As it was, Tibor and I jumped up on a desk while the dogs leapt and bayed at us. I can only assume they didn't attack because Kleiger had trained them to stay off tables.

Tibor yelled at the dogs to 'shoo!', which I found hilarious. I dissolved into near-hysterical laughter, which I then passed on to him; within a few minutes we were holding each other up while cackling insanely, which enraged the dogs even more, though thankfully *still* not enough to jump up onto the desks.

We were still laughing when we heard the voices outside.

To compound the error, we'd forgotten Kleiger actually lived in the same building, along with half a dozen of his bully-boys, all of whom were about to storm in. They couldn't have done us any actual harm, but then neither could the dogs. Unless – it occurred to us even in our fuddled states – one of them was Czobor, or one of them turned our own guns against us. So Tibor jumped to another desk, beside the window. For a chunky little guy he was surprisingly nimble and managed a perfect landing, although the way he flailed for balance when the desk seemed about to collapse slightly spoiled the effect. "Come on, Val!"

I jumped too, and we climbed out of the window. Which was where the next phase of our problems began.

There was a narrow windowsill, but no ledge extending from it round the building. Nor was there a fire escape or even drainpipe in reach. Meaning we either stayed on the windowsill, where Kleiger and company would see us right away, or we jumped.

Did I forget to mention the FDP's offices were on the third floor?

Long story short: we both ended up dangling from the windowsill by our fingertips while inside the office the dogs went wild and Kleiger and his men stamped and shouted.

"So, Val," Tibor whispered. "Any more brilliant ideas?"

I laughed so hard at that I lost my grip.

I broke both legs, along with several ribs, and possibly fractured my skill, so the next few minutes are little blurred even now. I've no idea how Tibor got down to street level without injuring himself, but he somehow did, before throwing me over his shoulder and taking off, pursued by Kleiger's outraged screams and the dogs baying from overhead. I was more or less healed by the time we got back to our apartment: the only lasting injuries were to our pride.

Such was the brief career of the *Gräfin* von Brandenstein-Vršovci, Gentlewoman Thief, and I doubt I'd do any better in the present day.

Luckily, I realise, there are other ways of finding out what I need to know.

Unlike the Empire I served, I've moved with the times; I've had to. As I moved from identity to identity, getting the necessary documents became trickier and more complicated. When I met you I'd been Valerie Varden for nine years, but had false IDs in another half-dozen names, just in case. Ensuring they were up to date and would pass inspection meant familiarising myself with certain aspects of the internet. Most notably the darknet.

The laptop already has a VPN installed; downloading a Tor browser takes minutes – after that I'm on my way. I find someone who can do what I need, agree a price – half upfront, half on completion – and arrange a bitcoin transfer.

And then I wait. I used to be good at that, but seem to have lost the skill. I pace, wishing I still smoked and could actually do so in the room; I consider ordering room service, then decide against it. I try to read, but the book's just jumbles of words that mean nothing. I throw it across the room, go back to pacing, then finally lie down, close my eyes, take deep breaths and try to clear my head. Mindfulness. Meditation. If I can just relax…

I'm cold and stiff, lying on top of the covers. The room's cold, and dark. I rub my eyes, groan and stir, fumble for my phone. It's a little after two a.m.

Another shower, then I put the kettle on. Herbal tea this time: camomile. Whenever I was stressed or upset, you always made me a mug. I drank it to humour you at first: I always thought it tasted like grass clippings. The cake you usually provided with it probably did more to help my mood. But grass clippings or not, the taste soothes me now: it makes me think of you grinning and raising your eyebrows, saying *Better now?* And of me rolling my eyes and saying *Yes Mum* in reply. Just for a moment I'm back in our front room, lying on the sofa with you, my head on your breasts. (Yes, that's a thing of mine, has been ever since Katrin. What can I do? I like what I like. And your breasts were lovely, so round and soft and deep. That stings suddenly, thin and sharp and piercing, like a meat skewer pushed into my flesh. There are tears in my eyes because I'll never rest my head there again.)

Once I've towelled myself dry, I get back under the covers but can't sleep; for better or for worse, I'm awake again. I make another camomile tea, pace some more, then yield to temptation. I open up the laptop, and log back in.

And on the darknet, my contact has come through. There's a link to download a PDF, and a message saying: *Money please.*

I download the PDF, transfer the funds, make a third cup of grass clippings and begin to read.

The digest my contact's put together is as thorough as it is clear. Viribus Unitis Security's one of a group of companies in Austria, Germany, Czechia and Slovakia. Another security firm in Prague, a property development company in Bratislava, a media conglomerate based in Salzburg, an archaeological institute in Žilina, scientific research labs in Graz and Karlovy Vary. A diverse portfolio, owned by a single parent company.

The other company names would have tipped me off just as surely as Viribus Unitis: the Bratislava property firm is called Cisársky, which means 'Imperial' in Slovak, and the Prague security company's Černý Orel, which is even more on the nose: it's Czech for 'Black Eagle'. In Karlovy Vary we have Radetzky Laboratories, while the Salzburg media combine's called Heldenberg – 'hero mountain' – the same as the memorial site where Field Marshal Radetzky, like so many Imperial generals, was buried. The archaeological institute's the Hötzendorf, which is starting to feel like outright trolling: Franz Conrad von Hötzendorf was the Austro-Hungarian Army's Chief of the General Staff in the Great War. And the research lab in Graz...

...is the Sindelar Institute.

The breath goes out of me, and I feel cold. The Sindelar Gate was located in Styria's Sulm Valley, and Styria's state capital is Graz.

But the Sindelar Gate was destroyed: once the last of the *Falkenjaeger* had been sent out, Emperor Karl had it blown to pieces. I don't know what happened to Dr Sindelar himself, or the creatures that guarded the Gate, but it's gone. It ensured there'd be no more immortals, just two undying armies, fighting the *Geheimkrieg* throughout eternity.

Do they *want* to be found?

The clincher is the parent company that owns it all: *Kronland GmBH*.

Crownland. As in *Black Eagles of the Crownlands*, to give them their full preposterous title.

Well, I always guessed I was more likely dealing with an old enemy than a former ally; not least because, for all I know, there aren't any other *Falkenjaeger* left. If my unit was the last, I'm now the only one.

There's the web: now for the spiders. I go straight to Crownland, since that's the centre of it all. This is where my enemy will be.

And there I find him, right at the top – quite literally. He's Crownland's MD and CEO: one Karel Jabůrek.

That name actually makes me laugh. My grandfather knew an old song from the Six Weeks' War and the Battle of Sadowa: despite being a sore loser, he wasn't completely without a sense of humour. The papers, he said, used to concoct ridiculously over-the-top tales of Austrian heroism in order to boost morale, so in the song, a valiant artilleryman, his arms blown off by enemy cannonballs, continues to load and fire his gun with his feet, even after his head's blown off too. The song's named after him: *Canoneer Jabůrek*. My enemy's got a sense of humour. Or perhaps he just liked having a name similar to his own.

Because my contact's thoughtfully captured photographs of the relevant personnel, too. And I recognise Jabůrek instantly. It's not like Varga, who was right in front of me without my recognising him for months. It's immediate, not least because the bastard hasn't changed a whit in over a hundred years. It could be the picture from his *Evidenzbüro* file.

I'm looking at a photograph of a dead man.

It's Janáček.

———

When Sandor Horváth wasn't teaching us (with his usual brutality) to fight and kill, he was teaching us about our enemies.

There were about thirty of them: for some reason they had a far better survival rate than the *Falkenjaeger*. I was one of a training group of fifteen who entered the Sindelar Gate. Five of us came out again: six, if you count the thing that slithered out after us screaming and had to be shot, but I try not to. Or think about who it might have been.

I don't know if they used some safeguard we didn't know about, if whatever was beyond the Gate favoured them somehow, or if it was just blind luck, but almost every Black Eagle survived the process. They got away, but at least we knew their names.

Names, faces, military records, family backgrounds, friends and associates. Not that we expected their former lives to be any use, but there was always the chance. Immortal or not, however steely their dedication to their cause, they were still human. It could certainly do no harm to know. And so we did: the *Evidenzbüro* files were very thorough. Unsurprisingly: I'd helped compile them myself.

We had front and profile shots of them all, plus any other pictures we'd been able to find. It's surprising how little people can resemble their official photos: remember how we used to giggle over your passport photo, how you said it made you look like a serial killer? It didn't, of course.

Horváth made slides of all the photographs, and three times a week at Aehrenbach he'd jumble them up to stage what we called – though not to his face – the Magic Lantern Show. He'd show slide after slide, and at his barked command a random trainee had to identify the subject, or tell Horváth what regiment the man had served with, when he'd joined the Black Eagles, how many brothers or sisters he had, what persons of current or former importance he was connected to, and so on. And on. Interminably.

"I don't trust written notes," Horváth told me once. "You're soldiers – allegedly – not fucking clerks. Won't have time to look in your notebook, Countess, not when you're in the thick of it. Just like Mummy and Daddy won't help you out when these sods are trying to blow your brains out. Know them! Know the bastards like you were screwing them every night, so that you can kill them. Next slide!" *Click.* "Right, your ladyship, who's this arsehole?"

"Major Neklan Janáček," I said. The man depicted on the slide had a narrow face, a brush of dark hair and a monobrow; a sharp dagger of a Roman nose; a pouting, almost feminine, Cupid's bow mouth; dark, sullen eyes. "Serbian Campaign, then the Italian Front." The Serbian Campaign, like Ulrich; the White War, like Franz and Conrad. "Then six months in the *Evidenzbüro*. Three brothers, one killed in Galicia – others serving with…"

And on, and on.

"Janáček," Horváth said. "Remember this one, boys and girls. He's the worst of the lot. And he knows how to kill."

So much for blowing his brains out in 1997, then. He's still out there. Rich, too: with fingers in pies all across the old Empire's heartland.

The worst of the lot, said Horváth, and he wasn't wrong. The original Black Eagles formed to arrest the Empire's decline; the second generation, like Janáček, who came aboard towards the end of the War, were recruited in order to build it anew. A tall order, given how it was splitting into a host of new nations, but they'd have forever to do it. And in addition to the time-honoured Habsburg qualities of cruelty and ruthlessness – though Janáček's actions during the Serbian Campaign alone had shown him more than capable of both – he was patient, cunning and a cold-blooded, capable planner.

The *Evidenzbüro* had almost been the only service the Black Eagles hadn't infiltrated, but Janáček had managed it, transferring in late in the war when most of the Black Eagles were dropping out of sight, salting away wealth and weapons and setting up communication networks. The *Evidenzbüro*, tasked with finding the men, the caches and the networks, was their biggest threat.

Planting an agent among us at that stage was an effective move, but an audacious and risky one. Janáček not only volunteered to infiltrate the *Evidenzbüro*, but made a brilliant job of it and fooled us till very nearly the last minute. When we suspected we'd been infiltrated, Janáček deflected suspicion to an officer called Bárányos, who then turned up very conveniently dead in an apparent suicide.

Luckily, a sharp-eyed *Evidenzbüro* officer (i.e. me) spotted a detail in the incriminating papers planted on Bárányos: a small, easy-to-miss error, based on which I quickly worked out the real traitor's identity. I took two other *Evidenzbüro* officers to Janáček's apartment to bring him in, under the pretext of wanting his help with the Bárányos papers, but either someone let something slip or his instincts warned him: he opened fire with a pistol, killing one of the men with me and maiming the other; I chased him, but he got away.

Even so, that little coup ensured I became a *Falkenjaeger*. Colonel Ronge, the head of the *Evidenzbüro*, made it clear to the powers-that-still-just-about-were-by-then that if not for me Janáček might have sabotaged the *Büro's* efforts even more effectively: we might never even have discovered the Sindelar Gate, or been in a position to use it ourselves.

I've wondered sometimes what would have happened if the Black Eagles had been able to quietly wait, unsuspected and unhindered, to plot the Empire's resurrection as originally planned. Without the *Falkenjaeger* to hound them, would they have reshaped the European map, or would they still have fallen away from their original purpose as they did with us in pursuit?

Over the years, *Falkenjaeger* units – mine included – came close to finishing Janáček, but he always got away. I did learn, however, via another Black Eagle we ran to earth in Greece, that of all the *Falkenjaeger*, Janáček feared and hated me the most. Bad enough I was a woman doing a man's job, and a 'filthy degenerate' to boot, but I'd nearly got him, right at the beginning, before he could walk the Gate. Exposed him when he'd thought himself safe. The ambush he laid in Istanbul in 1927 that killed Stefan and Mathias, had been meant for me; it was only by a last-minute chance that Mathias went instead.

I was glad I had that effect on him, because *Janáček* scared *me*. I admit I was glad when Varga told me he'd killed himself, because if any Black Eagle was actually capable of carrying out their original plan – or at least making an attempt that would cause havoc and destruction even if it failed – Janáček would have been the one.

Did Varga lie to me, or did he just not know? On balance, I think the second. Like me, Varga walked away from the *Geheimkrieg*, fighting only because the last of my old unit came after him. Varga had to kill Erick – and worse, Tibor, even though he'd no desire to. He hadn't wanted to kill me, either, and I didn't give him a reason to. Janáček would have despised Varga as Ulrich despised me: a traitor to the cause. Maybe that's why he faked his death, deciding his ex-comrades had turned too soft and weak to trust.

That, and it would have thrown the *Falkenjaeger* off the scent. Was he still afraid of me, even then? Is he still? It would explain everything: he'd watch out for old enemies, after all, and what happened in Manchester would have put me back on his radar. Maybe Berlin was just where he caught up with me.

Well, it's academic now: what matters is ending the threat. I could keep running: flee Europe and vanish into some disaster zone as planned, losing myself and resuming my old penance. But if I'm right, Janáček won't give up: he'll keep sending people after me until I'm dead.

The only question is where to find him.

I check through the pictures of Crownland's remaining key personnel, in case Janáček had company when he went underground, but there's no one I recognise. Just ordinary, boring mortals, far as I can make out.

I log back onto the darknet and arrange another job with my contact: where can I find Karel Jabůrek? I pay the deposit, then shut down the computer. Suddenly, at last, I'm very tired. So I turn out the lights, and settle down to sleep.

I wake up sometime after ten a.m. I didn't realise how exhausting the past few days have been. I ask room service to send up coffee and sweet rolls I shower and lounge on the bed in my dressing gown, a towel wrapped around my head to disguise how my hair's already growing back again.

A knock on the door: I answer it, keeping out of the line of fire, Roth-Steyr held ready under my robe. But it's only room service. I eat the sweet rolls, drink the coffee, then get ready to face the day, using the clippers to shave my head's back and side to a fine stubble, trimming the flat-top and refreshing the dye job before getting dressed. Around midday, I log back on to the darknet. My contact's come through again: I arrange payment, and download the information they've sent.

Karel Jabůrek has apartments in the capitals of all the countries Crownland operates in – Berlin, Prague, Bratislava, here in Vienna – but he isn't at any of them. He's at his primary residence: a private estate in the Salzkammergut, near the Traunsee, with state-of-the-art security and armed guards. I laugh, a short and bitter sound, when I see the name.

Aehrenbach.

———

As with Bradenstein, it's a shock to see the place has survived, even if my memories of it aren't as pleasant.

Again, I want to walk away from this, and vanish. I know that's what you'd tell me to do. And Louise, I want to, truly. But Janáček will follow. He won't give up. And he won't face me himself: he'll send someone to do it. And then someone else, and someone else, until the job's done. Now he knows I'm alive; now I've killed his men.

If he could only have forgotten his old fear of me, Hanna wouldn't have been shot. My three stalkers in Berlin would still be alive, and the people I killed at Bradenstein. All those people dead, just so I can stay alive. There's probably a point where it'd be better to let them finish me: fewer murders that way.

No. I can see you snort and shake your head, arms folded, the way you did whenever I said something foolish or self-pitying. *Don't talk shite, Val*, you'd say. *You were minding your own business, and they came after you. You didn't have any choice.*

But maybe that's wishful thinking. Given how much you never knew about me, how can I know what you'd really say if you did? It doesn't matter. I don't want to die. I'm not ready to put my gun in my mouth, or wait for another bunch of blacksuits to do it for me.

So, a hundred years on, I'm going back to Aehrenbach. I doubt it'll be as pleasant as my return to Bradenstein, and there'll be no room for any surprises.

Abruptly the hotel room feels claustrophobic and unsafe. All anyone need do is force the door and – I reach for the Roth-Steyr, then realise I've left it in the bathroom. The carelessness. Convinced the blacksuits are about to burst in, I run and grab the pistol, then move back to the bed, keeping the gun aimed at the door.

I'm shaking. What am I thinking of? I've one handgun, over a hundred years old. It's loaded with a fucking stripper clip, for Christ's sake, and holds ten rounds. Ten rounds of 8mm Roth-Steyr ammunition, too; hardly the world's most powerful cartridge. Far less potent than the 9mm bullets in a Steyr M9, or the 5.56mm rifle rounds in a Steyr AUG. Steyr, Steyr, always Steyr. How many people will be guarding Aehrenbach? It'll be in my contact's report; they're usually thorough. There'll be plenty, anyway. An army, waiting for me.

I remind myself the blacksuits had the same advantage over me at Bradenstein, and that I'm still here and they're not. It doesn't help. I was lucky; I caught them off-guard, attacking when they thought I'd run, and I took their weapons. At Aehrenbach, they'll be ready and waiting. Expecting me to try.

For one paranoid moment I wonder if Janáček might try tipping the police off about me – arrested and detained, I'd be unarmed and a sitting duck. But what if I resisted and they shot me? Just a short step then to letting the whole cat out of the bag, and he won't want that. No, he'll keep this private. Between us.

I study the report again. The priority now is to find a way in. I go back on the darknet and give my contact one more job: up-to-date schematics on the

Aehrenbach estate, the buildings and security layout. I remember the old place, of course, but there's no predicting what changes Janáček might have made. I can't afford any surprises: go in, find him, kill him, then get out and disappear.

I don't like doing this. I'm out of practice for this kind of killing. Before, it was self-defence, the heat of combat. This is different. Cold-blooded. Premeditated. This is murder.

Which I've done before. But then I walked away from it. I dedicated myself to healing instead of slaughter. And most of all, I met you.

In another life.

But it's got to be done.

And for that I hate Janáček now more than I ever have.

I lie back on the bed, the pistol beside me, waiting. Finally the computer pings; I open the files from my contact, send a payment and begin to plan.

———

I get in touch with someone else via the darknet and make the necessary arrangements – paying through the nose because it's a lot to arrange at short notice, but needs must. I transfer more funds, then sleep for a few hours: I need to be rested and alert. Around half past eleven, I slip out of the room, along with those items I need to travel with: I'm unlikely to be back. I leave some cash behind, to settle my bill. Whatever else I am, I'm not a thief.

The Radisson Blu has its own garage, and I make my way to a particular space, where a black 4X4's been parked. I crouch down and reach under the driver's door: the key-fob is taped there. I pop open the boot of the vehicle, and find a barrel-bag. I unzip it, just enough to glimpse the highly illegal arsenal inside, then zip it shut again, close the boot, get in the car and drive – out of the garage, and then out of Vienna.

I take the B38 to avoid the tolls, passing through Krems an der Dohau, Freistadt and Linz – home of my beloved Linzer torte, and of a certain Corporal Shicklgruber whose dreams of Empire had been no less grandiose in scale than the Black Eagles', the final collapse of which I witnessed first-hand in Berlin. Somewhere to the south is the town of Steyr, where the arms firm that manufactured my old pistol was founded. And further on, towards the end of my journey, the old town of Vöcklabruck, the gateway to the Salzkammergut, which also housed a sub-camp of the Mauthausen concentration camp where between a hundred and three hundred thousand people died.

History: the sheer bastard *weight* of it, sometimes. Especially if you're unlucky enough to be connected to it too intimately.

After Vöcklabruck, I turn off the Gmunden road, away from the Traunsee, and drive as deep as I dare along the narrow winding track into the woods surrounding Aehrenbach. When I'm about half a kilometre from where the motion sensors and alarm beams begin, I stop. Better to be safe.

Out of nowhere, I burst into tears. Stupid. Soft. Weak. I tell myself I'm a soldier; I'm *Falkenjaeger*. But that's the problem: for the first time in years, I really am. I'm no longer defending myself with my old skills: I'm a hunter, a killer. Executioner; assassin. I don't want to be. But there's no choice.

The crying jag subsides; I wipe my face, pop the 4X4's trunk again and unzip the barrel-bag – fully, this time. The first items I take out are a black jumpsuit, gloves and a balaclava. I put them on, and the effect's complete. Life is but a walking shadow; and now, so am I.

Then:

Item: One SafeGuard Coolmax bulletproof vest, 100% Kevlar.

Item: One Steyr AUG assault rifle, 5.56mm calibre.

Items: Two Steyr M9 automatics in a double shoulder holster, 9mm calibre.

Item: One Ruger Mk.IV 22/45 Tactical pistol with Silent-SR suppressor, .22 calibre.

Items: Four hand grenades: two shrapnel, two phosphorous.

Item: One Repetierpistole M.7, AKA Roth-Steyr, 8mm calibre, in a small of the back holster.

There wasn't time to perform the rituals I'd learned from Siczynski on the other weapons' ammunition, so the Roth-Steyr's the one gun I have that can actually harm Janáček. The other weapons, aside from the .22, are those the blacksuits used at Bradenstein: in a pinch I can hopefully steal some of their ammunition for an additional advantage. The .22's for stealth: with the silencer, the only noise is a metallic snapping sound, little louder than the click of a typewriter key.

Maybe I'll only need the Roth-Steyr; maybe I'll evade the sensors, avoid Janáček's men and only have to deal with the man himself, then get away clean before anyone notices what's happened.

Yeah, right. As you used to say in situations like this: *Oink, flap, oink, flap.*

I secure the pistols in their holsters, sling the AUG across my back and pull back the bolt on the .22, then step off the dirt track into the trees. It rained earlier, while I was driving west; I can smell the petrichor and the scent of damp pines.

One deep breath, savouring the scents and memories. And then I fall into a crouch and set off through the trees, pistol held steady. I'm no longer Valerie Varden, Valerie Steiner, or any of those other names. I'm not even the *Gräfin* Valerie Elisabeth Franziska von Bradensten-Vršvoci now. I'm *Falkenjaeger*, nothing more.

———

I'm maybe twenty steps into the woods when a dozen red dots swarm and hover in the centre of my chest like fireflies, then crawl up into my face. A cold voice, echoing from the surrounding trees, tells me to drop the pistol and raise my hands.

———

I'm at their mercy, and they've shown no sign of having any so far. But then they could have killed me without warning or a word. Instead of bullets, blacksuits come out of the trees, take my guns and cable-tie my hands behind my back.

My Roth-Steyr's shoved through someone's belt; I feel a pang, strangely bereft: that murderous hunk of steel's been the one constant in my existence since the Great War. Even when I didn't want it, it was there should I need it. I need it more than ever now, and it's gone.

They knew I was coming. They were waiting. Hidden cameras? Or were they watching me even in Vienna, despite all my efforts at evasion, just letting me walk into the lion's den?

And why aren't I dead? Janáček's been trying to kill me since Berlin, and he's not a Bond villain. He's cold, calculating, and won't detail his master plan while suspending me over a piranha tank (and piranhas would only piss me off, anyway.) What use am I alive?

I've a nasty suspicion, but do my best not to consider it.

The blacksuits march me to an open-topped Humvee, and I'm half-lifted, half-dragged into the back. I don't kick or struggle. No point. I haven't given up, but I won't get anywhere resisting yet.

The Humvee drives along a dirt track, weaving through a tunnel of close-packed firs. The reverent silence of the woods, the soft sounds of birds and small creatures in the undergrowth, is gone. There's only the engine. Petrol fumes taint the scents of damp earth and pine.

The track emerges onto a long white road. For half a minute the trees conceal everything around us but the night sky overhead, clear of all but a few final rags of cloud, alight with stars. Then the road curves round, opening out, and I can see Aehrenbach.

The big Baroque building looks a welcoming site: it always did. Aehrenbach was never a fortress, but a *Lustschloss* – a pleasure palace, a rural retreat for some noble family that died out around the end of the eighteenth century, passing first to the crown and then, during the Great War, the Army, who used it as a convalescent hospital until it was commandeered by the *Evidenzbüro* as a training facility. The central building is recessed and topped with a dome; long wings spread out on either side and press forward ahead of it. The façade is dark brown stone, a warm earth colour. Outwardly it looks no different; the big changes will be internal.

There's a high wall, and a gate. How had I meant to get over the wall? It no longer matters. If I could only get my hands free, they'd be doing me a favour.

Except I *can* get my hands free. However deep I tried to bury the *Falkenjaeger* in me, it was always there, watchful for anything that might serve me should the past refuse to stay as dead as I wanted it to. Freeing myself from a set of cable ties, should I ever be secured in them, is a skill I familiarised myself some time ago: when they secured my hands I clenched my fists tight and held them together, palms facing out. It's the simplest method: makes my wrists bigger, so that it's easier to slip out of the restraints.

But for now I'm surrounded by blacksuits who'll cut me down if I try anything. The moment, if there is one, hasn't come yet. I must believe it exists, that there's still a chance. The important thing's to recognise it when it's here.

Floodlights snap into life, illuminating the forecourt. Apart from their stark glare and the vehicle I'm in, this could be the night I first came here, with Ulrich and Tibor. Just the three of us; we'd meet the others soon enough. There were electric lights then, too, but nowhere near as bright: the glow had been warmer, gentler.

We were in a horse-drawn carriage that night. The road was rougher, too; the carriage rocked and bounced, wheels clattering over the rocky, uneven surface. I was sure something would break and send us flying. Ulrich sat staring out of the window, eyes empty.

That emptiness had been there since his return from the Serbian Campaign. Our armies had been repulsed by the Serbs again and again; they only won with German aid, and inflicted appalling atrocities as they went. Ulrich never told what had happened during his part of the war – what he'd seen and suffered, or what he'd done – and I hadn't asked him. I was afraid to find out. I only knew that after Serbia he was never truly himself again, never whole. Perhaps that was why he became so perfect a *Falkenjaeger*, while I, once so much like him, proved so unsuited to the role.

Beside me, Tibor squeezed my hand, but when I looked his usual smile was gone. We were crossing into unknown territory now, into an unknown land.

What would I have done if I could have seen ahead? Horváth was waiting at the end of it all: he marched down the steps, straight-backed despite his grey hair and seamed leather face. The weeks of brutal training; that last cruel initiation ceremony. And then the Sindelar Gate, and all that had lain beyond.

Given that knowledge I might have turned and run. Or tried, at least. If I had, I doubt I'd have got far. I'd known that from the start; it was one of the things that meant I obeyed Horváth and shot the dog. Having said yes, you were either *Falkenjaeger*, or someone who lacked the steel to be *Falkenjaeger*. And if you were lacking, you couldn't be trusted, and if you couldn't be trusted there could only be one ending.

No, by the night of the coach-ride it was already too late to change my mind. I'd have to have seen the future much earlier. Years of loss and destruction:

being bound up in them all, even complicit. Decades of trying to balance the scales with acts of conscience, never knowing if they were enough.

Finding you. That might almost make it all worthwhile. Three years out of over a hundred: that's how long it took me to learn what was precious.

And then having found you, losing you. And worse: having to bear responsibility for the loss, because Ulrich only killed you because of me.

Better I hadn't lived, really.

I shake my head, drawing glances from the blacksuits. The rifle barrel comes up, but another blacksuit knocks it aside. I almost startled them into shooting there. And we wouldn't want that, because whether I should have lived or not doesn't matter: I did, I'm still here, and there's still Janáček to deal with.

I'll settle with Janáček; then maybe I can die.

But not before.

The Humvee pulls into the forecourt, halting at the steps to Aehrenbach's main doors. Four blacksuits take up positions around the rear of the vehicle. The others bundle me out, keeping out of their comrades' lines of fire so I'm covered at all times.

I'm marched up the polished stone steps towards the great double oak doors of Aehrenbach, flanked by their barley-sugar columns below a cartouche displaying that long-dead family's coat of arms. The doors swing open and I half-expect Horváth to stride out, but nobody's there: they must be automated. Beyond is the entrance hall; marble floors, walls heavy with cartouches and *putti*, painted ceilings, and a grand stairway leading up.

Up the stairs we go, a Steyr AUG prodding me in either side, letting me know only a fool would try anything. I already know that; right now, I can't even work on the cable ties.

The moment will come, I tell myself; I must believe it'll come.

At the top of the staircase, there's a corridor, then a door, then another door behind that: a steel one, closed tight, a locking wheel in its centre. When they open it, cold white light spills out.

The blacksuits shove me through; one trips me and I go sprawling. It's not an act of spite. By the time I'm on my feet, they've slammed and locked the door behind me, scuppering any chance I might have had of escape.

Let that not have been the moment; let it still be to come.

The bare room's tiled in white: ceiling, floors and walls. Bright lights glare and dazzle off the surface. Sleeping here would be impossible. The only relief from the whiteness is the steel door, a mirror taking up most of one wall, and a steel and plastic stool. I look around for a moment, then stare at my reflection. I look pale and thin, no threat to anybody. I sit down and wait.

I expect the door to open, but in retrospect that's silly. Instead the mirror changes, growing transparent. The room behind it is more conventional-looking: wood-panelled walls, ornate gilded cornices, a desk and a chair. A cigarette box on the desk, a heavy table lighter beside it. There's also a microphone.

The desk's empty. After a moment, I hear the muffled sound of a door opening and closing, and a man in an expensive charcoal-grey suit and white silk shirt walks in. He sits down, pulls the chair close to the desk, then looks up at me through the glass with dark, emotionless eyes under a single bushy monobrow. He doesn't speak. I don't know what he's looking for but assume he finds it, because at length he nods and presses a button on the microphone. I try not to jump as a sudden crackle and buzz erupts from hidden speakers, but fail.

The faintest hint of a smile bothers the corner of his Cupid's bow mouth; then it straightens.

"Countess," he says, in English, with the barest hint of an accent. "What a pleasure."

"Janáček," I answer.

―――――

It shouldn't be a shock: after all it's only hours since I saw his photograph from the Crownland website. Yet seeing him there, in the flesh – even separated by a sheet of no doubt bulletproof glass – is still a jolt.

The last immortals I met were my brother, and Varga. One *Falkenjaeger*, one Black Eagle. Erick and Tibor, too, but they were already dead. Before that, decades had passed without encountering any others. Least of all Janáček.

We met once only, before either of us walked the gate. I didn't know Janáček personally when he was with the *Evidenzbüro*: we only came face to face when I tried to arrest him, and there was no time for conversation then. Ever since we've played the long game; me looking for him, him looking over his shoulder for me. Or at least he's played it, not knowing I'd resigned.

"You look very healthy," I say, "for a man who shot himself in 1997."

Again, his mouth comes close to a smile. "You stayed well-informed, I see."

I unclench my fists and press my palms tight together. The zip ties slacken – not much, but hopefully just enough. The key, the man who taught me this trick said, is to get your thumb free. "Varga told me."

"Before you and your brother killed him."

"I didn't kill Varga."

"Oh, your brother fired the shot, but…" Janáček gestures lazily, takes a cigarette from the box, lights it, leans back and breathes out smoke "…these things were always a team effort on your part."

"Not for a long time," I say. "Your intel's out of date."

This time it's a full-fledged smile, but sour. "Really."

"I left the *Falkenjaeger* in Berlin. 1945, right after I killed Czobor. I'd had enough."

"Of *course* you had."

"Believe it or don't, it's true."

"And it's nothing but pure coincidence, I suppose, that your brother and the rest of your *zug* happened to appear alongside you in Manchester when poor Varga was killed?"

I shrug and pull a face; it masks a twinge of pain from the joint of my left thumb as I struggle to worm it free. "I know how it sounds, Janáček. I do. But it happens to be the truth."

He looks at me through the glass, with that mocking smile. I think of Hanna and the bodies I left in Kreuzberg and at Bradenstein; none of it would have happened if not for Janáček and his paranoia, and suddenly I'm angry. "For Christ's sake, Janáček, people quit. Even immortals. Varga did, didn't he?"

The smile becomes a grimace. "Ferenc *was* a disappointment. Weak. So many of them were.

Couldn't take the *pressure*. So they deserted. Thought that would save them. Didn't, though, did it? Look at poor von Hortzweig. Threw it all over – even became a *Communist*, of all things. Risked life and limb fighting the Nazis, and what happened? You and your brother, again. Two shots in the head, and an unmarked grave."

"You're pretty well-informed yourself."

Now Janáček shrugs. "They deserved no better. Weakness, Countess. Surprised Varga lasted as long as he did. It became very clear to me some time ago I couldn't rely on my so-called comrades, only myself."

He puffs on his cigarette; again I almost wish I still smoked. "That why you pretended to kill yourself?"

"What choice did I have? The others had just… I mean, *Varga*. Of all the Black Eagles of the Crownland, I thought I could trust him. Thought he had *balls*. *Steel*. But no. Just another coward. Another traitor. As I said, I was *very* disappointed."

"He could have killed me, and didn't," I say. "And he wasn't soft. He killed Erick von Kulmer and Tibor Thököly." My voice catches on Tibor's name, to my annoyance. None of this will do me the slightest good, but while Janáček and I are talking he isn't trying to kill me; I'll damn well *try* at least to reach him, however little chance I have.

Besides, it gives me time to work on the cable ties. I can feel I'm making progress.

"Oh, yes. Thököly. Fond of the little queer, weren't you?"

I try to look bored; it's the best response to petty goading like that. "Varga let me live. I let him go. My brother killed him, on his own. And I killed Ulrich."

Janáček actually laughs. "Oh, that's *rich. Really* rich."

"He killed my partner." I want to say *wife*; *partner's* a new word, unlikely to strike half the chord with Janáček as *wife*. I wish I *had* married you. we talked about it, but weren't in any rush. We should have been, in retrospect. "And he was going to kill me. To him, I was a traitor. I was quicker, that's all. Shot him in the throat, and then I blew his brains out." My voice doesn't shake when I say that, although it's close. When I killed Ulrich I told myself he wasn't my brother any more, that he was a different person to the one I'd known. But he was and he wasn't. It's hard to untangle my happier memories of him from how it ended. Especially after what he did. You, tied to the armchair, a bullet in your head.

"Fairy tales," says Janáček. "A good cover story, though. I'll give you that."

I'm close to freeing my thumb from the ties, but I'm already tired of this game. It's hard work, telling the truth when people won't believe you: the urge to needle him's too sharp and sudden to resist. "I forgot how scared you are of me."

The smile disappears as though slapped off his face. "I'm not scared of you."

"You just faked your own death to hide from me."

"Don't flatter yourself, Countess. Caution's not the same as fear. I couldn't rely on my so-called comrades, and I knew you weren't giving up."

"Except I did. In '45."

He titters. "Of course you did, Countess. Still, it worked."

"Until you spoiled it by trying to kill me."

"Can't really blame me for that. You were always good at falling off the radar. I knew you'd vanish again."

"If you'd left me alone, none of this would have happened. I was going away." Africa, Asia, the Americas. Some continent beginning with A. Other than Antarctica, obviously: the cold wouldn't kill me, but even I have my limits.

"Of course you were. All the better to resume the hunt."

"God's sake," I mutter. "Change the record."

"You covered your tracks well," he says, "but you're *experienced* at that, aren't you, Countess? Had quite a job, picking up your trail. Nearly lost you in France. But then up you pop in Berlin, eating dinner with a pretty little darkie at the Grill Royal."

Pretty little darkie: he'd have called you that, too, given I picked Hanna for her resemblance. Which reminds me what happened to Hanna. Which reminds me, once again, what happened to you. I think he sees something in my face, because he stops smirking and straightens up in his chair.

"Yes," I say quickly. Keep him talking. A couple more minutes. "Nearly had me too. Except you employ idiots."

Janáček's face tightens. My left thumb finally comes free of the cable ties; I try not to let my triumph show.

"I mean, you couldn't mix the two of us up. A mixed-race woman and a white redhead. But the fuckwits you sent shot the wrong one, didn't they?" I lean forward, speaking slowly. "I wouldn't have even *known*, Janáček. Is that sinking in through your fucking solid-bone head, yet? If you'd left me alone, you'd have been fine. Or if you *had* to come after me, if your fuckwits just *got it right*, I'd never have known what hit me. As it is, look at this fucking mess, eh?"

"You're forgetting I have you, Countess. It all worked out in the end."

But it's not the end, not yet. Not that I'll remind him of that lest he hurries that ending along, before the moment arrives, the one that'll give me my chance. "Just about," I say. "Third time lucky, I suppose. No – fourth, isn't it? Yes. First your baboons shot Hanna instead of me. Then they tried again, and I killed them." I sound as dismissive as I can, not letting myself remember what I did. I can't afford a conscience, not yet. Maybe not ever. "And then Bradenstein. Twenty-odd you sent, that time, all geared up, and all I had was my old Roth-Steyr." I laugh, hard, keeping eye contact. My left hand is free of the cable ties now; I've hooked my little finger through them so they don't fall to the floor when my right hand comes free as well. "And I killed them all, Janáček. Is that what you're gonna rebuild the Empire with? Retards like that?" I hate that word, but know it'll needle him. And it's working: his jaws are clenched, a muscle twitching in his cheek.

But while I try to find another barb to throw, Janáček leans back and smiles. "I'll admit I could have hired people who were... of more proven ability? But the problem with mercenaries is you can only trust them insofar as you pay them, and if someone offers them more – well, who knows? Whereas men and women dedicated to a cause..."

"Got it," I say. "Might be useless, but they're loyal."

"Some are better than others. But we'll get there."

"Suppose I should admire your optimism." I really wish I had a cigarette: I could look far more impressive smoking. "From what I've seen so far, you might manage to take over a couple of streets in Salford in about ten years' time."

"I'm not as caught in the past as you think, Countess. Once we have an Empire again, we can exercise force to protect it, from enemies without and within. But first we've got to build it. And to make that happen, people have to *want* it."

"Good luck with that."

"No luck required, Countess. Just time. Which the likes of you and I definitely have. You know why the Empire fell apart?"

"I'm sure you'll tell me." Decadence, immorality…

"Democracy and nationalism. Those were the big two. Instead of being content to be part of the Monarchy, people wanted to be free of it. Now, that's a hard battle to win. But you can turn your enemy's strengths against them. Look how things are falling apart, Countess. Democracy's self-destructing, and nationalism? It's everywhere."

I snort, but feel cold. "You trying to claim credit for all that?"

"All? Of course not. But some? I like to think I helped things along their way. Big media conglomerates can do that. Decide which stories to focus on and which not to. And when you've money, you can spread the wealth around – the right politicians, the right organisations. Look at the state the EU's in. Five, ten more years and it'll be gone. Guaranteed. Never takes much to spark things off in the Balkans – the Greeks and Turks, or the Serbs and just about everybody else. And then there's Russia. Ukraine, the Baltic States, Poland, Hungary, not to mention the Germans – if they aren't afraid of the Russkies now, they soon will be. Another decade or two, the whole continent'll be on fire, and they'll beg for a strong leader to pull things together again. Freedom doesn't mean much when you're afraid for your life."

The worst of it is, he isn't wrong. We saw it ourselves, both of us, between the wars, in so many countries. Even so: "You really think you can just march one of the Habsburgs back into Schönbrunn and that'll be it, the Empire's back?"

"Oh, it might not be *called* the Empire, or the Monarchy. Not at first. That's just a label. Labels change. A couple of generations, and who knows? Besides, the trappings don't matter, the reality does. And the reality will be an Empire, across all *Mitteleuropa*. Bigger and better than ever."

My hands are now both free, but I keep them behind my back as if still bound, the cable ties held between the forefinger and thumb of each. The moment isn't here yet, but it's close. "And what about Russia? And America? You think they'll just stand by and—"

"Oh, they'll have problems of their own. Already do, in fact. China's the only one to really worry about, but we can keep them occupied for a year or two at the critical time."

Full-blown megalomania, and it should be ridiculous. But the conflicts and divisions he's describing are all too believable. Whether Janáček's played as big a role in sparking them as he thinks doesn't matter. He sees the trends, widens the cracks, funnels money to those who'll exploit them as he prefers. His master plan's chances of success aren't important: just *trying* to realise it is capable of killing millions. I remember both World Wars, the carnage and devastation from them and their aftermaths, and they were fought – till the very end of the Second – without nuclear weapons. If Russia and America collapse, some crazed general or politician could easily push the button in a final petty act of spite: *If we can't have the world, no one will.* And so many – too many – other countries have such weapons too…

And if the worst came to the worst, if all the Earth was irradiated wasteland in which nothing could live, who'd remain? Only Janáček and I. Along with any others of our kind, but I've a horrible suspicion we're the last.

Although if I don't act I won't be the last anything much longer. Janáček's not waiting ten or twenty years to finish me. Ten or twenty minutes might be a stretch.

Time to bait him again. "Got it all planned out, haven't you? A lunatic and an army of halfwits. What a comedown. Poor Emperor Karl would have a fit if he could see—"

Janáček's jaw clenches. "That traitorous milksop. Who cares what he—"

"Well, I doubt old Franz Joseph would have been impressed either. I mean, come on – I know the Army was no great shakes in 1914, but your lot make them look like the three hundred Spartans."

Janáček's bright red, half-rising from his seat. But then he breathes out, and sits back down.

"Clever," he says. "Clever, clever, Countess. *Wily.* Always were. Typical woman. Like that little cunt Marie Vetsera. She started it all – got her hooks into Prince Rudolf and…"

The old Black Eagle mantra. Marie von Vetsera, Crown Prince Rudolf's mistress: supposedly killed in a 'suicide pact' with him at Mayerling, in fact murdered by the Black Eagles, who blamed her for leading Rudolf astray. They'd hoped the Prince would mend his ways. Instead he shot himself, thus helping ensure their precious Empire's collapse.

But the world's Janáčeks never bother with inconvenient facts. He blathers on about poor little Marie Vetsera and women in general before returning to me. "You're trying to provoke me. Get me to do something foolish, like coming in there. But it won't work. And you won't anger me into killing you."

I'd a horrible feeling he'd say that.

"You're not dying yet, Countess. We've eggs to harvest. We need more immortals."

Can't complain, I suppose, if being the only female to walk the Gate saved me from being shot in the woods. Not that there's any proof I'm even fertile, although the old monthly curse has persisted[2].

Janáček pushes a button on his desk. There's a buzz, and from the doorway I hear the locking wheel start to turn. "I just wanted to talk to you," he says, "before the end. Seemed only right, after all these years. But now we're done."

The door opens. I press my wrists together, so no one can see they're free.

Two blacksuits come in. I'm almost insulted. There'll be more nearby, of course. But for now, just two. I can handle that.

Both have the usual kit: rifle, pistol, knife in boot. Blacksuit One advances across the room towards the chair; Blacksuit Two stays in the doorway, covering me.

I hold my wrists together. I hold my wrists together. This is it.

The moment.

---

[2] Yes, I know: a hundred years of PMS. I've heard all the jokes, and none of them are funny. V von B-V.

———

"There'll be a moment," Horváth told us, in the ballroom at Aehrenbach. He sat in a chair, hands tied behind his back. As always the air was cold and damp, with a smell of mildew I thought I'd never get out of my lungs. "If you're captured, held prisoner, whatever it may be, there'll be a moment they fuck up. They'll be looking the wrong way, or off-guard, or they'll think you've given up. Always, in any situation, a moment you can exploit so you come out alive. Now fucking shoot me, Thököly."

Tibor strode forward, raising his Steyr-Hahn. By then he'd learned to obey Horváth, even when he ordered something so apparently insane, not least because Horváth was always one step ahead. This time, though, I couldn't see how he could lose. I guessed the guns were loaded with blanks, but you could never tell with him.

Tibor put his gun to Horváth's head, and Horváth barked "Mistake!" Even as he said it, Tibor was lying on the wooden floor, Horváth's foot on his chest and his gun in Horváth's freed hands.

"Too close," said Horváth. "Not enough to kill me, was it? No, you wanted me to *squirm*, didn't you, eh? Thought I'd shit myself. Well, I didn't. And look at you now."

Tibor glared up at him in mute hate, and Horváth grinned back, never taking his eyes from Tibor's as he spoke. "He hates me, this one – don't you, *buzoralo*?" He ruffled Tibor's hair with his free hand. Tibor thrashed, trying to throw him off, but Horváth cocked the pistol. "Ah-ah," he said. "Behave, little boy."

Oh yes, Tibor hated Horváth. Horváth really had it in for him – thought, maybe, that being queer made him a weak link. Well, Tibor proved him wrong. So did I – although I'd expected a harder time still, being a woman. But in his warped, weird way, I think Horváth cared for me, and showed it by toughening me up, giving me the tools to survive. Maybe that was his game with Tibor, too. If so, I suppose it worked. There's no denying that.

"He hates me," repeated Horváth, "so he wanted to make me suffer. Maybe even make me beg. And that's when he fucked up. Got too close. And when he did – bam!"

He tossed the Steyr-Hahn to the floor. We all jumped – not just Tibor – but it didn't go off. Dud rounds; not even blanks. Should have guessed.

"Maybe they hate you," said Horváth. "Maybe they think you're beaten. In your case, Countess..." he glanced at me "...they might have something else in mind. Unless they're like this one here, and then it's the rest of you need to worry." He grunted a laugh, took his foot off Tibor's chest and feinted a kick at his ribs. Tibor scrambled to his feet, red-faced, crouched as if to leap at the Sergeant.

"Give it a go if you fancy," said Horváth. "No? Right then. Pick up your gun, get back in place." He turned back to the rest of us. "One way or another, that moment will come. What decides whether you getting out of whatever fucking mess you've landed yourself in or not comes down to two things. First one's recognising when the moment's there. Get it wrong and you're dead. Second one's knowing what to do when it comes along."

Horváth turned his chair around and straddled it, folded arms resting on the back. "The second bit's the one I'll teach you first. All the little moves and tricks. But they're fuck-all use without the first skill. I can tell you what to look or listen for, but the only way to be sure's to feel it. And that part's trickier." He grinned. "So it'll hurt. A lot."

And it did. But in the end I learned, and better than any of the others.

Blacksuit One grabs my collar and pulls me to my feet, his rifle in my ribs. Halfway to the door I drop the cable ties and spread my arms to knock the gun aside, then snap my head back into his face. His nose breaks; my right hand finds his hip holster, and the grip of his Steyr M9.

Blacksuit Two opens fire almost at once, but not quite; I throw myself sideways and down as she pulls the trigger. The burst meant for me knocks Blacksuit One across the room. But I'm holding his pistol.

I pull back the slide in case the chamber wasn't loaded: a bullet spits out of the breech to confirm it was. Blacksuit Two steps into the room, sweeping her AUG towards me; I pull the trigger twice. She cannons back into the doorframe and falls out into the corridor, firing into the ceiling.

In the mirror, Janáček stares at me. Then he bolts. I empty the Steyr at him, but I was right about the mirror: the glass cracks and splinters but doesn't break.

I throw the gun at the doorway as another blacksuit comes through. He ducks and his shots go wild, hitting the walls and ceiling and filling the air with a haze of pulverised ceramic. I grab Blacksuit

One's rifle and fire: the third blacksuit staggers into the corridor. I run to the doorway as a fourth blacksuit catches hold of him and cut them both down.

Well, what did you expect? Mercy?

I take Blacksuit Two's belt and pistol and forage spare magazines for both guns. A klaxon starts blaring. I run down the corridor and turn right. At the corner of the next corridor along, blacksuits are swarming, and I open fire before they see me.

Shouts, screams, running footsteps. A grenade bounces along the carpet. I pick it up and throw it back, not afraid at all: everything's very fast and very slow, all at once. The grenade detonates. There are more screams.

I run to the corner and peer round. The walls are on fire and there are bodies everywhere. A knot of blacksuits falls back along the corridor, laying down a barrage with their assault rifles. More grenades explode; the hallway fills with yellow fumes and my eyes burn. Smoke and tear gas. I glimpse blacksuits donning respirators before the rifle fire forces me back into cover; I fire a burst around the corner and hear a cry.

Janáček's in the middle of those blacksuits. I've no way of knowing if his masterplan can continue without him, but doubt it: his ego's too big. Janáček's Crownland and Crownland's him. Cut off the head, kill the body.

None of which will necessarily save the world, or Europe, from the catastrophes he prophesied: they could easily have been taking shape without him. and might still. But I can stop him profiting from them if nothing else. And – more selfishly – ensure my own safety.

I run through the smoke, keeping low, eyes burning from the tear gas. Two blacksuits lie dead in the hallway; one, thank whatever gods there are, wears a hooded gas mask. I take it and pull it on.

———

There were a cluster of outbuildings on the estate, abandoned even before the war. One afternoon, Horváth set up a machine-gun on the roof of the tallest building and opened fire while we blundered through clouds of tear gas below him.

Gas warfare, after all, had become a fact of life. A horrible, vicious way to fight. I never forgot hearing about the 'Attack of the Dead Men,' when the Germans attacked the Osowiec Fortress with chlorine and bromine gas, only to be driven back by Russian soldiers vomiting up their own blood and lung-tissue. Walking the Gate would keep us alive if that happened, but pain, blindness and lungs full of bloody muck were potentially fatal handicaps if a Black Eagle was lying in wait.

Horváth hung gas masks from nails hammered into the outbuildings' walls and posts. He released the smoke and tear gas first; we had two minutes before he followed them up with chlorine. And all the while he was shooting at us.

I told myself he'd aim to miss, but we lost two men that day: a boy called Alfred took a round in the head and died instantly, while Oskar, the oldest candidate, didn't find his mask in time. He was still alive when the ambulance took him away, but we never saw him again.

I remember my eyes burning, tears streaming down my face, and the flat yammer of the gun. The thwack and crack of bullets hitting earth and stone. Dust and splinters stinging my face. Then getting the gas mask on, just in time, begging the pain in my eyes to stop as I crawled for cover and slowly watched the air turn green.

Horváth had been subdued, afterwards. "That's what fucking happens when you're too slow, boys and girl," he said, then stomped off. Maybe his conscience troubled him a little. Or perhaps he *had* been aiming, however narrowly, to miss, and Alfred's death had hurt his professional pride.

———

The dead blacksuits are carrying grenades, too. An idea starts to form.

They're shouting up ahead. Around the next corner I see the remaining blacksuits shepherding Janáček towards a lift at the end of the corridor. I lob a smoke grenade towards them, duck back from the hail of gunfire, then underarm a second grenade, this one a shrapnel charge, through the smoke. It explodes: after that there are only screams and shooting.

I toss another smoke grenade, hit the ground and crawl. Bullets fly overhead. I grit my teeth and keep going till I reach the first dead blacksuit, then twist round and empty my rifle down the corridor in short bursts while pushing myself back along the carpet through the smoke.

Hands grab me, pull me to my feet. "You all right?"

"Yeah."

Just as I'd hoped: with my black jumpsuit, coupled with the respirator hood, I've been mistaken for one of their own in the confusion. I stumble along the corridor with my helper, inserting a new magazine into the AUG. Two more blacksuits fire past us into the smoke. Janáček's already in the elevator. We crowd in after him, the doors slide shut and the lift descends.

Mirrored walls, so it looks as though I'm surrounded by a horde of Janáčeks and blacksuits. According to the lift's control panel, there are three more floors: ground, basement and sub-basement, and we're heading for the last.

The lift stinks of sweat, fear and gunsmoke. There are drops of blood on the floor, and half a dozen bullet cases.

"I want reinforcements brought in," snaps Janáček. "Surround the house, comb the grounds for that bitch. And I want a full detail on me. Call in the chopper, pick me up from—"

He stops. For a moment I wonder why. Then I feel how the atmosphere in the lift's changed, and realise the others are moving back, away from me.

Janáček and the others have removed their masks. Of course they have. Now they're away from the smoke and gas, the masks get in the way: they restrict the vision, muffle the voice. Janáček, two men – one black, one white – and a thickset woman with a brutal face and broken nose.

Janáček's holding a pistol; not just any pistol, but a Roth-Steyr. *My* Roth-Steyr: I recognise the scratches around the barrel that have been there since 1942. The 8mm hole at the business end suddenly looks very wide. My own gun. The final insult. "Take your mask off," he says.

I throw myself sideways and bring up the AUG, but the black man and the woman are on me, and then Janáček fires. In the narrow space the shot makes my ears whine. A mirrored wall explodes in shards of flying glass; a four-inch cut opens under the woman's right eye but she barely flinches, even as blood streams down her cheek.

They force the rifle barrel down, trying to pull it from my grip. The white blacksuit moves in to help, pinning me against the wall. Janáček's back against the far wall, brandishing the Roth-Steyr, shouting orders no one can hear for the ringing in their ears. I manage to draw up one knee, planting a foot against the wall behind me, then boost forward, hard as I can, thrusting the AUG towards the blacksuits, then letting go. They cannon into Janáček and I kick-scramble backwards into the far corner from them, clawing for the M9.

Janáček screaming, raising the Roth-Steyr. The woman's AUG comes up.

Through the whining in my ears, I hear a faint 'ping'.

I pull the M9's trigger and keep doing it till all eighteen rounds are gone. The air fills with smoke and broken mirror-glass. I'm vaguely aware of screams. Blood and flesh and bone explode up the shattered walls.

The woman flops sideways, out of the lift, blocking the doors as they start to slide closed. Her face is gone, burst like rotten fruit. The other two blacksuits lie tangled together. I can't hear. The floor's a slush of blood, glass and cartridge cases; the grey hazy air stinks of sulphur. And Janáček's gone. One of the dead blacksuits is missing his pistol.

I reload the Steyr. The lift doors half-close, then reopen. Outside is cold light and polished white floors. I crawl to the doors and peer out.

High ceilings, white light. The sub-basement at Aehrenbach used to be a wine cellar – one of the best in the Empire, someone told me once, although by the time we used the place it was an underground shooting range. The lack of natural light meant it could be used to simulate almost any conditions, which Sergeant Horváth used to take great pleasure in doing – usually 'night, in heavy rain'. Bastard.

It had an earth floor then – great fun when it was 'raining' – and was generally filthy, crawling with spiders and rats. Now it's as white and tiled as the room I was interrogated in, which makes me wonder what else Janáček had in mind for me, especially when I see the glass cases gleaming under the antiseptic light.

I combat-roll from the lift to the nearest case, just as a steel shutter crashes down, missing my heels by centimetres and slicing the dead woman in two. A bullet ricochets off the shutter; the other hits the glass case, although it leaves nothing more than a white mark: bulletproof glass, as in the interrogation room. I fire back, three rounds rapid. Silence.

"Janáček?" I call.

Nothing. Perhaps I hit him, but I doubt it.

I edge around the glass case, doing my best not to inspect the contents, which I think were human once. While I've seen nothing like it before, it reminds me of the thing that slid out of the Sindelar Gate after the rest of my group. One of Janáček's less fortunate companions, maybe. I presume it's dead. Or hope so.

There are rows of glass cases in the sub-basement space, but few of the contents are organic. Many contain stone fragments studded with sapphire-like gems and carved with glyphs. It takes a few seconds, given the circumstances, to recognise them: they're pieces of the Sindelar Gate.

"Janáček?" I call again.

No answer, but I'd have been foolish to expect one.

I wonder what the Sindelar Institute, up in Graz, has in its possession. No doubt Janáček owns the Sulm Valley site where the Gate originally stood. Maybe he's hoping to rebuild it, and make a new generation of immortals that way. He certainly seems determined to do so, and without my ovaries that would have been his only option. Thankfully he doesn't seem to have had any success, hence (presumably) his plan to harvest my innards for the cause. Small mercies, I suppose; at least I haven't a cadre of would-be Janáčeks to contend with. Then again, babies might suit him better: he could indoctrinate them from birth about the old Empire's glories and the holy cause of its resurrection.

I move between the glass cases. Along with fragments of the Gate, they're full of archaeological relics: pieces of rock, ceramic or bone, or parchment made (I hope) from animal hide, inscribed with characters in dead tongues, or crude pictograms whose meaning I'd rather not speculate on. Something about a painted figure in one case, and a crudely carved stone one in another, catches my eye. The shape in each case is tall and thin, humanoid but most definitely not human; the one in the painting looms over the stick-figure people around it. Its head's irregularly shaped, asymmetrical – not from any lack of artistic technique, but because it accurately represents whatever it's modelled on. It has what could be either eyes or mouths, but there are too many of them, and they're all different sizes.

But it's the hands that grab my attention. They have too many fingers, and all end in long curved talons, and something's horribly familiar about that. I tell myself to look away, that my real concern's Janáček, but then I turn and come face to face with the original.

Laid out in the biggest case of all, it's twelve feet tall and still clad in its dark, ragged robe, its too-many-fingered hands – bluish-coloured, with their ivory-yellow talons – protruding from the cuffs. The robe's cowl is flung back to reveal the front of the head – it doesn't exactly have a face. The apertures in it are most definitely mouths, though, and not eyes. They're lined with row on row of spine-like teeth.

I haven't seen this thing in over a century, but it's a difficult sight to forget: one of the Monks who guarded the Sindelar Gate. And not just any Monk: most of them – whatever they were, wherever they came from – were only eight or nine feet high. Only their leader – their High Priest? – was this tall.

And now, apparently, it's dead: a stuffed exhibit in a museum case. Or perhaps it's only sleeping, as it presumably slept away the centuries in the Sulm Valley tumulus before Sindelar woke it up.

Where's Janáček? It's a miracle he hasn't sneaked up on me and blown my brains out by now. By way of an answer, there's an explosion that tears a section of the sub-basement wall away; the air fills with smoke. A blurred shape rushes at the hole, firing as it goes. I duck to avoid the bullets; when I come back up, the shape's gone.

Janáček's running. Of course he is; I'm the one he's afraid of, after all.

Originally he'll have meant to hide. No doubt more blacksuits from Viribus Unitis or some similar outfit are en route. The steel shutters should have sealed him safely in, with armed guards around him, to wait me out, but now the sanctum's breached, and he's alone.

I sprint to the hole; beyond it is a tunnel with those now-familiar white-tiled walls. An escape route, presumably. There are lights, but I can't see Janáček for smoke and dust. I go in, keeping low, and wish I hadn't discarded the gas mask.

A dull thud, and the floor ahead explodes into shards and powder. The concussion slams me flat against the wall, fragments slice and riddle me, but they're just ordinary injuries, easily repaired. I drag myself forward, then get up and stagger; finally I run, head down, weaving, throwing myself from side to side. My only chance is to close the gap as fast as I can: get too close on Janáček's tail for him to safely detonate another charge. And to keep *him* running: while he's running, he can't shoot at me.

The tunnel's full of smoke, but I can see a shadow, up ahead – weaving too fast, too blurred in the smoke, to chance a shot at. But I keep going. No pain now; all the wounds are healed. There's only the pursuit. I am *Falkenjaeger* now, a purpose and nothing more, closing on my prey. The moment will come.

———

"Never run in a straight line under fire," Horváth said, as we all lay groaning on the sub-basement floor. He'd only been armed with a pair of revolvers, but had bested a group of half a dozen trainees. The revolvers had been loaded with wax bullets: non-lethal, but they hurt like Hell's own fury. "A straight line's predictable, and there's nothing some bastard with a machine gun likes better. Only has to move the muzzle just ahead of you and DAH-DAH-DAH-DAH-DAH!"

He grinned, pleased with his Maxim gun impersonation. "And then your aristo brains'll be splattered up the nearest wall. No great loss to humanity in any of your cases, mind you, but you're not allowed to die till you've done your bit for His Royal and Apostolic Majesty. Very impolite otherwise. So you fucking *weave*, Countess. And you, von Kulmer," he told Erick, who was nursing a full half-dozen bruises from the wax rounds, "stay fucking low, assuming a beanpole like you's capable. You *do* fold in the middle, don't you? Well, try it, because next time they won't be fucking wax."

Horváth held up three fingers. "The golden rules, when moving under fire: keep changing course, keep low, and above all, *keep fucking moving*. Otherwise you might as well just paint a bullseye on your arse, so the other sod knows where your brains are."

All good advice, especially the last part: Janáček only stops and fires at the very last, when he reaches the ladder at the tunnel's end. Another dull thud, more smoke and dust: explosive bolts to blow the exit open. He scrambles up the ladder, rapid-firing a Steyr M9 as he goes.

I drop and roll to avoid the bullets and manage to fire one shot back. Janáček drops the pistol, though I don't know if it's because he's hit or because it's empty. Probably the second, because he's climbing even faster now. And then the rising smoke swallows him.

I keep firing as I run to the ladder – I don't expect to hit him, but he still has my Roth-Steyr – and climb up after him. When I emerge from the exit blasted in the turf above I open fire again.

My gun's empty, but so are the woods around me. Out of the hatch and roll for cover, in case of any more booby-traps, or another steel shutter slamming into place. My belt has one spare magazine for the M9, so I reload.

No sign of Janáček, but there are shouts and cries in the distance. When I look, I see why: Aehrenbach is burning.

Maybe one of the grenade explosions started a fire and it's spread, or Janáček's initiated it to cover his escape – because, in the end that's all that matters as far as he's concerned. Fuck those who serve him: he is the cause and the cause is him.

Which just shows he never understood what he was about. Say what you like about Emperor Karl, or even that old arch-reactionary Franz Joseph: they understood duty. They had obligations, not just privileges.

Maybe all Janáček's big dreams had a built-in self-destruct mechanism, in that sense. But it was never about whether they could be realised: it was about how many people he'd kill in the attempt to do so.

Flame and smoke's pouring from Aehrenbach's windows. The whole place is burning. One more piece of my past. The Janáčeks of the world promise to preserve and to restore, but never do: in reality, they'll gladly destroy all they claim to love for their own aggrandisement, till only ashes remain.

My anger brings the forest floor into sharper focus: even in the dark, with only the light of the burning house to see by, it's not remotely hard to find Janáček's trail through the trees. It's as clear now as if Horváth was beside me, his hand on my neck, turning my head to follow his finger, rasping instructions into my ear.

Staying low, gun held ready, I move from tree to tree. The crackle of flames dies away and there's only the woods' cool darkness and soft scent. It's soon too dark to really see at all; instead I listen for snapping twigs and rustling undergrowth, hunting by sound.

One way or another, this ends tonight.

<hr>

Horváth was a country boy: it was practically the only piece of personal information he ever let slip. "Back on the farm we'd cut a dozen pigs' throats before breakfast and not lose our appetite, *buzoralo*," he'd bark at Tibor. "Couldn't be dainty there! We did what we had to, and you'd better too, or I won't give the Black Eagles a *chance* to kill you."

I'd had one other brief glimpse of who Sandor Horváth had been before the Army claimed his soul, and it'd been here in the woods of Aehrenbach.

Occasionally we were allowed a few hours of leisure time; in one of them, I went into the woods. It was autumn: rustling russet leaves, the smell of damp earth. I'd thought I was alone, till I heard someone first whistling, then singing:

"Fekekte föd, fehér az én zsebkendöm,
Elhagyott a legkedvesebb szeretöm…"[3]

<hr>

[3] "Black is the earth, white is my handkerchief. My lover has abandoned me." He sang it with a good deal of feeling, too. Hard to believe he ever had a heart, let alone ever had it broken. Maybe he was singing about a gun. V. von B-V.

I'd padded through the trees and found one of the brooks that ran through the estate. Horváth was on one of the higher banks, his back against a tree-stump, tossing pebbles into the water. His collar was loose, his feet bare; his boots and socks lay beside him on the grass. It was the only time I saw him look at all relaxed, at least for the instant before he realised I was there.

We studied one another in silence. Then Horváth said "Fuck off, Countess," and threw another pebble in the stream.

The following day, he began taking us into the woods – individually, or in pairs – to teach us how to read a trail. I was always part of a pair; Horváth clearly didn't want to discuss that unguarded moment. I never spoke of it, nor mentioned it to any of the others, not even Tibor. I don't know why.

Finally, he taught us to hunt in the dark.

For that final exercise, Horváth went into the woods at night alone and a pair of us would try to hunt him down. We all carried old Rast und Gasser revolvers – the very model my father killed himself with – loaded with wax bullets, again ensuring that defeat, while painful, would not be lethal. A good thing, too: Horváth always won.

I was paired with Albin; the two of us spread out as we tracked Horváth through the woods, ten or fifteen metres apart. Then suddenly, through the trees, a hoarse voice said "Bang!" and I dived for cover. I blew two short whistles – a signal Albin and I had worked out between us – but there was no response, and I realised I was now hunting alone.

I cocked my revolver and waited, but no attack came. When I was sure Horváth had moved away,

I found his trail once more, aware I was now both hunter and prey. Twice I heard footsteps behind me and dived for cover, aiming into the dark, but no one was there – once I almost caught a moving shadow in my sights, but that was all.

He stopped trying to stalk me after that, and I heard him moving further and further ahead. I guessed his intention: he was going to retreat to a position where he'd have the advantage, and wait for me to come to him.

I trailed him through the woods until I heard running water: it was the stream I'd found him beside that day. I could even see the high bank he'd been sitting on and knew, with absolute certainty, he'd be waiting for me there. I circled around, downstream and downwind, then climbed into the deep channel of the brook, hunching as far below the level of the banks as I could.

It took time to reach his position, stealth being far more important than speed. Or comfort, for that matter; despite my leather boots, my feet were almost numb from the cold water. But patience is the greatest of all virtues when you're hunting, and eventually I was beneath Horváth's embankment. I grinned to myself when I saw a revolver's barrel protruding over the edge, clenching my teeth so they didn't chatter. I'd been right. Horváth was waiting for me, but didn't know I was already here.

I holstered the Rast und Gasser, climbed up the embankment until I was directly underneath him, then inched sideways to the closest dip in the bank before peering over. Horváth lay prone in the moonlight two metres away, wearing a woollen hunter's cap, gun extended in both hands. Slowly I brought my own pistol to bear, aimed at his head, and squeezed the trigger.

Properly speaking, it was closer than was safe for the wax bullets, but I was lost in the excitement of the moment. Even so, the result was something of a shock: Horváth's head flew clean off his shoulders, bounced off the bank and splashed into the water. In the same instant, cold metal pressed against my temple, and a voice whispered "Bang."

That came as even more of a shock, I will admit – enough of one that I lost my footing and fell with a yelp and crash into the stream, which, below that high bank, was deeper and colder than anywhere else along its length.

"You're dead, Countess," grinned Horváth, standing on the bank above me in his underwear, a second Rast und Gasser at his side. "Now up you get, before you freeze."

He retrieved his clothes from the dummy on the embankment, grumbling about the loss of his hunting cap, which had fallen in the stream and been washed away. Then we made our way back, me squelching in my boots, dripping wet and half-frozen, Horváth smoking one of his rare cigars. Neither of us spoke, until we reached the edge of the woods.

"Did better than any of these other arseholes, anyway," he said. "Nearly had me, Countess. But nearly's no good. Not in this game."

He clapped his hands and strode ahead. Albin sat waiting for us, a pile of cigarette butts between his feet. "Right, then," said Horváth. "Back home, children."

We walked back to Aehrenbach in silence.

I hear running water now, but it's a different brook and a good thirty metres to my left, while Janáček's trail lies directly ahead. My skin's prickling; it feels hypersensitive, aware of every breath of wind, the touch of every hanging leaf.

A very different hunt this time. Automatics instead of revolvers, and firing lead, not wax: there'll be no walking back to the house afterwards tonight. And no house, not any more. But most of all, there's no time.

Janáček's people are coming for him, and however well I know the woods I can't fight them all. Even if they don't kill me, they'll take him far away and hide him somewhere beyond my reach, and he'll wait there till I'm dead. He's got the resources to keep hunting: his people will keep coming even if I'm half a world away until the job's done, unless Janáček's no longer there to send them. If I don't kill him now, then today, tomorrow, or in a year, Janáček kills me.

The trail leads me to a clearing with a knoll in the centre, crowned with a huge ragged tree-stump and wormed with arm-thick roots. I remember the tree, I think, from when I trained here, and wonder when it came down.

The knoll is the perfect hide, giving Janáček a clear three-hundred-and-sixty-degree view of his surroundings. I squint at the grass and brambles atop the knoll, trying to find him, but he's too well-hidden, especially in this dark and at this range.

In the distance, I hear a helicopter.

Even Horváth would grind his teeth at this. The only way's to reach the knoll itself. Once there, if I can get in close enough, I can finish him – if I'm fast enough, agile enough. *Val be nimble, Val be quick, Val blow the head off this absolute dick.*

Not a bird flutters; not an animal moves. There's the faint crackle of flames as Aehrenbach burns, the brook's soft chuckle, and the sound of the helicopter, slowly growing nearer.

I break cover and run, head down. Go right, go left, then right again. Only six or seven metres from treeline to knoll, but all so open, so exposed. Any second there'll be a muzzle flash, before the bullet splits my skull.

But he doesn't fire, and the knoll rushes up to meet me. I fling myself down in among the roots and do my best to burrow into the earth. When I look up, I see it: a pistol, just poking clear of the grasses at the top. A short-barrelled revolver of some kind.

I keep still, trying to plan the next move. But what's Janáček doing? The gun hasn't moved.

It's a small gun, I realise: a .32, at most. The kind you'd carry in an ankle holster, to use at point-blank range, because with a barrel that short you'd never hit anything further away. A back-up piece, not your main weapon. Which is strange, because Janáček has my Roth-Steyr: a bigger, far more accurate gun. Why isn't he using that?

But I already know, of course, and in that moment of realisation time thickens to a crawl. And yet I move normally. I roll to my side so I face left, towards the brook, because of course that's where he's gone, so the sound will mask his movements. And as I do, Janáček steps out from behind a tree, aiming the Roth-Steyr in both hands. Even in the shadows among the trees I see his pale face and white silk shirt, grimed with dirt and other people's blood.

A long slow moment; a fragment of a heartbeat where it could go either way. He's squeezing his trigger and I'm squeezing mine, and it's all a matter of who's squeezing harder or faster, who started squeezing a moment before the other one, which gun has the lighter trigger. So many different variables at play, a dozen rolling dice. And by the blindest of blind chances, my M9 fires first.

The bullet takes Janáček in the chest and he goes back one stumbling step. I fire again, but he stays on his feet, still trying to bring the Roth-Steyr to bear. Feeling very calm now, I get up on one knee, aim and fire twice more. Janáček jerks bolt upright, falls back against a tree and his legs give way.

He's still breathing – ragged, hoarse and wet, blood and air bubbling in his shattered lungs – but he doesn't move. He's still holding the Roth-Steyr, but his fingers are limp. I go towards him, aiming at his head; when I'm about a metre away, his eyes roll up towards me. He tries to speak, but whatever he wants to say I'll never hear: all that comes out is bloody froth.

Suddenly I'm exhausted. I don't even hate him any more. I steady myself against another tree and sit down beside him, my joints creaking with what feels like every one of their hundred and thirty-ish years.

Janáček, wheezing and bloody-mouthed, stares at me.

"It was all true, you know," I tell him. "Everything I said. Every word. There was no big plan to get you. I was just minding my own business in Berlin. Didn't even know you were still alive. If you'd left me alone, none of this would've happened. None of it."

Janáček stares, and finally – too bloody late for it to do any good – I think he believes me. His eyes close, his shoulders shake, and a sort of knocking sound comes from his bloody, froth-clogged throat. At first I think he's crying, but then realise it's laughter.

"Yeah," I say. What else can be said now? "Yeah."

Janáček opens his eyes and looks up at the night and takes a deep breath. Maybe he means to say something, or to laugh again, or just to let out a long weary sigh at the absurdity of it all. But instead he shivers, and then his head falls forward. His eyes stay open, gazing without sight. And with a faint thin whistling sound, like a leaking balloon, that last breath trickles out of him again.

The chopper comes and goes; I hide in the woods till it and the rest of the blacksuits are gone, then make my way back through the woods, carrying my Roth-Steyr with me.

They left Aehrenbach to burn; left the house and all the dead, even Janáček himself, as soon as they realised they were too late. They'll cut their losses and disappear now, taking anything that isn't nailed down and won't take too long to shift or sell. With Janáček gone, it all falls apart: the whole shadowy empire, the whole mad dream. Some of the separate parts might still function after a fashion, still do some damage, still seep their poison to some extent. But they're not my problem.

Aehrenbach's roof has fallen in and one of the walls has collapsed; inside it's like a furnace, a mouth full of roaring flames, showering sparks up into the black sky. I'm about to go when I see movement. I stop and wait, and something stumbles out of the fire.

Most of its robe is burned away, but the High Priest seems otherwise unharmed. It raises its hands above its head in triumph, then blunders away, disappearing into the woods. Maybe some homing instinct's drawing it back to the Sulm Valley and the old burial mound, and whatever home it might still find there.

———

"So you're safe now?" Conrad says.

"I think so." We're sitting outside the summerhouse by the lake at Bradenstein, a week later. I look out across the water and wonder if I'll have time to take a boat out to the island before I go. I might never have the chance again. "How are you?"

"All right, I suppose." He looks at his hands. "I have bad dreams, sometimes. Nightmares."

"I can imagine."

I feel as though there's much more I should say to him, but don't know what. Hopefully I'll work that out, before I leave tomorrow.

For now, one quiet evening at my childhood home, one night's sleep in my old room, will be enough.

Earlier, browsing the local news in Berlin, I found a brief article saying that Hanna Neumann, the victim of a recent shooting incident, has been discharged from the Franziskus-Krankenhaus and is now recovering at home with her wife and children. I could trace her, with a little effort on the darkweb; get her number, or her email.

But what would I say? That I'm sorry? That she was caught in the crossfire of an old, dead war? That I wish her well? They'd all be true, but saying those things would heal nothing, not even my conscience. The best gift I can give Hanna is to go far away from her, so that our lives will never touch again. The same with Conrad.

"Where will you go?" he asks.

"I fancy Marrakesh," I say. "I've never been anywhere in Africa. I'll start there. After that, who knows?"

He nods and is silent. The lake's a flat calm mirror in the dusk; birds call faintly. I remember when it seemed an ocean, and Bradenstein the universe; when I couldn't conceive anything beyond it. Couldn't imagine the Empire it formed one tiny part of, let alone the world.

The world – a mote in space's endlessness though it might be – is vast; more than enough for me to hide in for another decade, another lifetime. But I'd be happy in one little corner of it, Louise, if I could only share it with you.

In another life.

I sip the wine Conrad's poured, and watch the sun go down. Tonight, Bradenstein, one last time; tomorrow, a train to Marseille and then a hired boat, out into the waiting world. And I'll be gone as if I never was, taking nothing with me but a Roth-Steyr automatic and a little oval portrait of you and I, under glass. They're all I need.

I'm good at leaving things behind.

Acknowledgements

As well as being the most loving, understanding and supportive partner any writer – or any person, full stop – could as for, Cate Gardner listened to me read this entire manuscript to her, which makes her a candidate for sainthood.

Emma Bunn beta-read the whole thing and provided feedback. Thank you as always, awesome cat lady.

Ladytron provided a most excellent the soundtrack with their album *Gravity The Seducer*.

I'm not well-travelled, so I'm very grateful to various friends and colleagues who helped with the details of the various countries and cities Val visits in the course of this tale. Any details that ring true are thanks to them; any errors are mine alone.

Lynda Rucker and Steve Toase shared their memories of Berlin.

Priya Sharma helped put me in touch with Erik R. Andara for information on Vienna. I also got to make the acquaintance of his adorable dog, Melvin the supermodel, if only in pictures on his Facebook feed.

Andy Caine put me in touch with Klara Smolova, who provided details relating to Prague, Czechia in general and the horrors of the D1 in particular.

My profound gratitude goes out to Rachel Verkade at The Future Fire Reviews, Matthew Cavanagh at Runalong The Shelves and Thomas Joyce at This Is Horror for their kind reviews about *Roth-Steyr*.

Last but far from least, my thanks go out to the gentle giant that is Steve Shaw at Black Shuck Books, both for publishing *Roth-Steyr* and for allowing me to continue Val's story here.

THE THREE BOOKS

by

Paul StJohn Mackintosh

"I've been told that this is the most elegant thing I've ever written. I can't think how such a dark brew of motifs came together to create that effect. But there's unassuaged longing and nostalgia in here, interwoven with the horror, as well as an unflagging drive towards the final consummation. I still feel more for the story's characters, whether love or loathing, than for any others I've created to date. Tragedy, urban legend, Gothic romance, warped fairy tale of New York: it's all there. And of course, most important of all is the seductive allure of writing and of books – and what that can lead some people to do.

You may not like my answer to the mystery of the third book. But I hope you stay to find out."

Paul StJohn Mackintosh

"Paul StJohn Mackintosh is one of those writers who just seems to quietly get on with the business of producing great fiction... it's an excellent showcase for his obvious talents. His writing, his imagination, his ability to lay out a well-paced and intricate story in only 100 pages is a great testament to his skills."

—This is Horror

blackshuckbooks.co.uk/signature

BLACK STAR, BLACK SUN

by

Rich Hawkins

"Black Star, Black Sun *is my tribute to Lovecraft, Ramsey Campbell, and the haunted fields of Somerset, where I seemed to spend much of my childhood. It's a story about going home and finding horror there when something beyond human understanding begins to invade our reality. It encompasses broken dreams, old memories, lost loved ones and a fundamentally hostile universe. It's the last song of a dying world before it falls to the Black Star.*"

Rich Hawkins

"Black Star, Black Sun *possesses a horror energy of sufficient intensity to make readers sit up straight. A descriptive force that shifts from the raw to the nuanced. A ferocious work of macabre imagination and one for readers of Conrad Williams and Gary McMahon.*"

—Adam Nevill, author of *The Ritual*

"*Reading Hawkins' novella is like sitting in front of a guttering open fire. Its glimmerings captivate, hissing with irrepressible life, and then, just when you're most seduced by its warmth, it spits stinging embers your way. This is incendiary fiction. Read at arms' length.*"

—Gary Fry, author of *Conjure House*

blackshuckbooks.co.uk/signature

DEAD LEAVES

by

Andrew David Barker

"*This book is my love letter to the horror genre. It is about what it means to be a horror fan; about how the genre can nurture an adolescent mind; how it can be a positive force in life.*

This book is set during a time when horror films were vilified in the press and in parliament like never before. It is about how being a fan of so-called 'video nasties' made you, in the eyes of the nation, a freak, a weirdo, or worse, someone who could actually be a danger to society.

This book is partly autobiographical, set in a time when Britain seemed to be a war with itself. It is a working class story about hope. All writers, filmmakers, musicians, painters – artists of any kind –were first inspired to create their own work by the guiding light of another's. The first spark that sets them on their way.

This book is about that spark."

Andrew David Barker

"*Whilst Thatcher colluded with the tabloids to distract the public... an urban quest for the ultimate video nasty was unfolding, before the forces of media madness and power drunk politicians destroyed the Holy Grail of gore!*"

—Graham Humphreys, painter of *The Evil Dead* poster

blackshuckbooks.co.uk/signature

THE FINITE

by

Kit Power

"The Finite *started as a dream; an image, really, on the edge of waking. My daughter and I, joining a stream of people walking past our house. We were marching together, and I saw that many of those behind us were sick, and struggling, and then I looked to the horizon and saw the mushroom cloud. I remember a wave of perfect horror and despair washing over me; the sure and certain knowledge that our march was doomed, as were we.*

The image didn't make it into the story, but the feeling did. King instructs us to write about what scares us. In The Finite, *I wrote about the worst thing I can imagine; my own childhood nightmare, resurrected and visited on my kid.*"

Kit Power

"The Finite *is* Where the Wind Blows *or* Threads *for the 21st century, played out on a tight scale by a father and his young daughter, which only serves to make it all the more heartbreaking.*"

—Priya Sharma, author of *Ormeshadow*

RICOCHET

by

Tim Dry

"*With* Ricochet *I wanted to break away from the traditional linear form of storytelling in a novella and instead create a series of seemingly unrelated vignettes. Like the inconsistent chaos of vivid dreams I chose to create stand-alone episodes that vary from being fearful to blackly humorous to the downright bizarre. It's a book that you can dip into at any point but there is an underlying cadence that will carry you along, albeit in a strangely seductive new way.*

Prepare to encounter a diverse collection of characters. Amongst them are gangsters, dead rock stars, psychics, comic strip heroes and villains, asylum inmates, UFOs, occult nazis, parisian ghosts, decaying and depraved royalty and topping the bill a special guest appearance by the Devil himself."

Tim Dry

Reads like the exquisite lovechild of William Burroughs and Philip K. Dick's fiction, with some Ballard thrown in for good measure. Wonderfully imaginative, darkly satirical – this is a must read!

—Paul Kane, author of *Sleeper(s)* and *Ghosts*

blackshuckbooks.co.uk/signature

ROTH-STEYR

by

Simon Bestwick

"You never know which ideas will stick in your mind, let alone where they'll go. Roth-Steyr began with an interest in the odd designs and names of early automatic pistols, and the decision to use one of them as a story title. What started out as an oddball short piece became a much longer and darker tale about how easily a familiar world can fall apart, how old convictions vanish or change, and why no one should want to live forever.

It's also about my obsession with history, in particular the chaotic upheavals that plagued the first half of the twentieth century and that are waking up again. Another 'long dark night of the European soul' feels very close today.

So here's the story of Valerie Varden. And her Roth-Steyr."

Simon Bestwick

"A slice of pitch-black cosmic pulp, elegant and inventive in all the most emotionally engaging ways."

—Gemma Files, author of *In That Endlessness, Our End*

A DIFFERENT KIND OF LIGHT

by

Simon Bestwick

"When I first read about the Le Mans Disaster, over twenty years ago, I knew there was a story to tell about the newsreel footage of the aftermath – footage so appalling it was never released. A story about how many of us want to see things we aren't supposed to, even when we insist we don't.

What I didn't know was who would tell that story. Last year I finally realised: two lovers who weren't lovers, in a world that was falling apart. So at long last I wrote their story and followed them into a shadow land of old films, grief, obsession and things worse than death.

You only need open this book, and the film will start to play."

Simon Bestwick

"Compulsively readable, original and chilling. Simon Bestwick's witty, engaging tone effortlessly and brilliantly amplifies its edge-of-your-seat atmosphere of creeping dread. I'll be sleeping with the lights on."

—Sarah Lotz, author of *The Three, Day Four, The White Road* & *Missing Person*

blackshuckbooks.co.uk/signature

Also from BLACK SHUCK *Signature*

THE INCARNATIONS OF MARIELA PEÑA

by

Steven J Dines

"The Incarnations of Mariela Peña *is unlike anything I have ever written. It started life (pardon the pun) as a zombie tale and very quickly became something else: a story about love and the fictions we tell ourselves.*

During its writing, I felt the ghost of Charles Bukowski looking over my shoulder. I made the conscious decision to not censor either the characters or myself but to write freely and with brutal, sometimes uncomfortable, honesty. I was betrayed by someone I cared deeply for, and like Poet, I had to tell the story, or at least this incarnation of it. A story about how the past refuses to die."

Steven J Dines

"*Call it literary horror, call it psychological horror, call it a journey into the darkness of the soul. It's all here. As intense and compelling a piece of work as I've read in many a year.*"

—Paul Finch, author of *Kiss of Death* and *Stolen*, and editor of the *Terror Tales* series.

blackshuckbooks.co.uk/signature

THE DERELICT

by

Neil Williams

"The Derelict *is really a story of two derelicts – the events on the first and their part in the creation of the second.*

With this story I've pretty much nailed my colours to the mast, so to speak. As the tale is intended as a tribute to stories by the likes of William Hope Hodgson or H P Lovecraft (with a passing nod to Coleridge's Ancient Mariner), where some terrible event is related in an unearthed journal or (as is the case here) by a narrator driven to near madness.

The primary influence on the story was the voyage of the Demeter, from Bram Stoker's Dracula, *one of the more compelling episodes of that novel. Here the crew are irrevocably doomed from the moment they set sail. There is never any hope of escape or salvation once the nature of their cargo becomes apparent. This was to be my jumping off point with* The Derelict.

Though I have charted a very different course from the one taken by Stoker, I have tried to remain resolutely true to the spirit of that genre of fiction and the time in which it was set."

Neil Williams

"*Fans of supernatural terror at sea will love* The Derelict. *I certainly did.*"

—Stephen Laws, author of *Ferocity* and *Chasm*

blackshuckbooks.co.uk/signature

AND THE NIGHT DID CLAIM THEM
by

Duncan P Bradshaw

"The night is a place where the places and people we see during the day are changed. Their properties — especially how we interact and consider them — are altered. But more than that, the night changes us as people. It's a time of day which both hides us away in the shadows and opens us up for reflection. Where we peer up at the stars, made aware of our utter insignificance and wonder, 'what if?' This book takes something that links every single one of us, and tries to illuminate its murky depths, finding things both familiar and alien. It's a story of loss, hope, and redemption; a barely audible whisper within, that even in our darkest hour, there is the promise of the light again."

Duncan P Bradshaw

"A creepy, absorbing novella about loss, regret, and the blackness awaiting us all. Bleak as hell; dark and silky as a pint of Guinness — I loved it."

—James Everington, author of *Trying To Be So Quiet*
and *The Quarantined City*

blackshuckbooks.co.uk/signature

Also from BLACK SHUCK *Signature*

AZEMAN
OR, THE TESTAMENT OF QUINCEY MORRIS
by
Lisa Moore

"How much do we really know about Quincey Morris?

In one of the greatest Grand-Guignol moments of all time, Dracula is caught feeding Mina blood from his own breast while her husband lies helpless on the same bed. In the chaos that follows, Morris runs outside, ostensibly in pursuit. "I could see Quincey Morris run across the lawn," Dr. Seward says, "and hide himself in the shadow of a great yew-tree. It puzzled me to think why he was doing this…" Then the doctor is distracted, and we never do find out.

This story rose up from that one question: Why, in this calamitous moment, did the brave and stalwart Quincey Morris hide behind a tree?"

Lisa Moore

———•———

"A fresh new take on one of the many enigmas of Dracula – just what is Quincey Morris's story?"

—Kim Newman, author of the *Anno Dracula* series

blackshuckbooks.co.uk/signature

Also from **BLACK SHUCK** *Signature*

SHADE OF STILLTHORPE
by
Tim Major

"It's fair to say that parenthood has dominated my thoughts – and certainly my identity – for the last nine years. While I love my children unconditionally, I'm morbidly fascinated by the idea of parenthood lacking an instinctive bond to counter the difficulties and sacrifices of such a period of life. And I'm afraid of any possible future in which that bond might be weaker.

Identity is a slippery thing. More than anything, I'm scared of losing it – my own, and those of the people I love. Several of my novels and stories have related to this fear. In Shade of Stillthorpe, it's quite literal: how would you react if your child was unrecognisable, suddenly, in all respects?"

Tim Major

A seemingly impossible premise becomes increasingly real in this inventive and heartbreaking tale of loss."

—Lucie McKnight Hardy, author of *Dead Relatives*

"Parenthood is a forest of emotions, including jealousy, confusion and terror, in Shade of Stillthorpe. It's a dark mystery that resonated deeply with me."

—Aliya Whiteley, author of *The Loosening Skin*

blackshuckbooks.co.uk/signature

SORROWMOUTH

by

Simon Avery

"For a long time Sorrowmouth existed as three or four separate ideas in different notebooks until one day, in a flash of divine inspiration, I recognised the common ground they shared with each other. A man trekking from one roadside memorial to another, in pursuit of grief; Beachy Head and its long dark history of suicide; William Blake and his angelic visions on Peckham Rye; Blake again with The Ghost of a Flea; a monstrous companion, bound by lifes' cruelty...

As I wrote I discovered these disparate elements were really about me getting to some deeper truth about myself, and about all the people I've known in my life, about the struggles we all have that no one save for loved ones see – alcoholism, dependence, self doubt, grief, mental illness. Sorrowmouth is about the mystery hiding at the heart of all things, making connections in the depths of sorrow, and what you have to sacrifice for a moment of vertigo."

Simon Avery

―――•―――

"Sorrowmouth is a story for these dark days. Simon Avery summons the spirit of William Blake in this visionary exploration of the manifestations of our grief and pain."
—Priya Sharma, author of *Ormeshadow*